How to Date a Rockstar

Cash & the Sinners #1

D.E. Haggerty

ISBN: 9789083368252

Also By D.E. Haggerty

Bragg's Truth

Bragg's Love

Perfect Bragg

Bragg's Match

Bragg's Christmas

My Forever Love

Forever For You

Just For Forever

Stay For Forever

Only Forever

Meet Disaster

Meet Not

Meet Dare

Meet Hate

A Hero for Hailey

A Protector for Phoebe

A Soldier for Suzie

A Fox for Faith

A Christmas for Chrissie

A Valentine for Valerie

A Love for Lexi

About Face

At Arm's Length

Hands Off

Knee Deep

Molly's Misadventures

Chapter 1

Indigo – A woman who does not suffer fools, especially when he's in her shower

INDIGO

The sign welcoming me to Winter Falls comes into view and the tears I'd barely managed to wrestle under control burst from my eyes once again. With my hands shaking, I pull to the side of the road. Grief, shame, and loss pour from me as I stare at the sign.

Why didn't I visit Grandma for the past five years? Yes, Mom forbade me, but I'm a grown woman. I don't have to follow Mommy's rules anymore.

And why didn't Grandma tell me she was sick? It's not as if we weren't in touch. We spoke every Saturday morning while I drove to yoga class. She told me all the gossip in Winter Falls – who got caught skinny dipping at the river, who snuck off to White Bridge for a 'secret' date everyone knew about, what sexy book the book club was reading – but she never said a word about having cancer.

Now Grandma's gone and I'm here to settle her estate. Clean out the house Grandpa built for her and sell it. I took a leave of absence from teaching since Mom still refuses to step foot in Winter Falls.

I don't know what Mom's problem is. While I was growing up, we came to Winter Falls every summer. It was magical. Swimming in the freezing river, playing softball with the other kids, sleeping in a tent in Grandma's backyard, and Grandma teaching me how to bake, although never her apple pie since the recipe was 'top secret'.

But then I graduated from high school, and Mom and Grandma had their big fight. Grandma never would tell me what it was about. Neither would Mom.

To be honest, I never expected Mom to tell me a thing. I'm not exactly her confidant considering her goal in life is to form my life exactly the way she wants it to be. My goals and wishes are irrelevant.

Meow!

I glance back at my kitty in her cage in the back seat. She bats at the bars.

"You wouldn't have to stay in the cage, Katy Purry, if you didn't try to drive all the time."

Meow!

"I'm going already. Geez."

Katy Purry is one demanding cat. I'm not kidding when I say she sits on my lap when I drive and tries to steer the car.

I park on the street in front of Grandma's house since she doesn't – didn't – have a driveway. Most houses here don't since cars are practically banned. Winter Falls' claim to fame is being the first carbon neutral town in the world. Which means cars with internal combustion engines are not allowed. Most people use golf carts to get around.

I stare at the Colonial house. The wraparound porch where I fell and skinned my knees when I was fleeing the kitchen with a piece of stolen apple pie. The hunter green exterior Grandma insisted I paint and re-paint until she was satisfied with my brush strokes. I had green paint in my hair for the first month back at school.

And the bright red front door smack dab in the middle of the house. The closed front door. In the past, when I pulled up to the house, Grandma's door would be wide open and she'd be standing in the doorway waving at me to hurry up and get inside. Not this time.

I inhale a deep breath and force myself out of the car. I open the rear door to release Katy Purry from her cage. She immediately jumps out and into my arms.

"You ready for this, Katy Purry?"

Meow! Meow!

Uh oh. Those are 'I'm hungry. Feed me now, peasant!'-meows.

I scratch her neck as I walk to the front door. "I bet Grandma has some nice tuna for you."

I'm lying. Grandma would never have canned tuna in her house. The one time I asked why, she gave me a lecture about dolphins and mercury and I don't know what. I was five. I never asked for a tuna sandwich again.

I try the door. As I suspected, it's unlocked. People in town don't usually lock their doors. Not when 'Winter Falls is the safest town in the world'.

The scent of cinnamon and apple hits me the second I enter. It smells as if Grandma has been baking her famous apple pie all afternoon. But she hasn't. She'll never bake her delicious pies again.

I—

Hold on. Do I hear water running? I listen closely. I do. There's water running somewhere upstairs. So much for the safest town in the world.

I clutch Katy Purry to my chest. She must sense my apprehension as she doesn't fight me. There's a first time for everything.

I creep up the stairs making sure to skip the third step. It squeaks and always got me in trouble when I tried to sneak out of the house. That was before I learned to climb out of my window onto the tree in the backyard.

I reach the landing and pause to listen. Dang it. There is definitely water running in the bathroom.

Did Grandma leave the bath on? I nearly snort. What am I thinking? The people of Winter Falls would notice if an empty house was using extra water. Unnecessary water usage is a sin in this town. Think I'm kidding? Ask me why I have a scar on my chin sometime.

Which means someone is in Grandma's house. How dare they? Who thinks they can use my grandma's house when she hasn't been gone a week?

I march to the bathroom and burst through the door. Steam fills the air preventing me from seeing much of anything, but I can make out an outline of a person on the other side of the shower curtain.

Someone's using Grandma's shower without her permission? Not on my watch.

I yank the shower curtain open. "What do you think you're doing?"

The man whirls around. His eyes widen when he sees me. As do mine.

This can't be happening. I must have fallen asleep on the plane from San Diego to Denver. No way is *he* in my grandma's bathroom. Cash Evans. The rockstar sensation of *Cash & the Sinners*. And my high school sweetheart who dumped me on graduation day.

I pinch myself and yelp. Darn it. I'm awake. This is really happening. My life sucks.

Cash Evans is in my grandma's shower. I can't help but notice he's no longer the boy I fell in love with. He's a man. Those gray eyes that used to sparkle when he looked at me are now bracketed by laugh lines. And the bump on his nose from a brawl he had after a concert is new.

The boy I knew couldn't grow a beard, but this man standing before me has several days of growth on his chin and cheeks. The look suits him.

My gaze travels further down to his chest. Oh my. The skinny boy I gave my virginity to no longer exists. This man is all muscle. My fingers tingle with the need to touch him. To feel every single inch of his skin. To test how strong those muscles are.

My heart speeds up and warmth spreads throughout my body at the memory of nights spent in this man's arms.

What are you thinking, Indigo?

This is not the boy I fell in love with. He's now a man. A man I don't know. The boy I knew no longer exists. He hasn't for a long time.

I growl at Cash. "What are you doing here?"

Katy Purry snarls at him.

Cash points to my kitty. "What the hell is that thing?"

I cuddle her close. "This is Katy Purry."

"Katy Purry?" he spits out. "You named your cat after a pop star? A pop star?"

"Do not start with me. My musical taste is not up for discussion."

He snorts. "Taste?"

I stomp my foot. "We are not discussing what music I listen to. We are never discussing what music I listen to. The question here is: what are you doing in my shower?"

He gulps. "Your shower?"

"Have all those concerts caused hearing loss?" I tap my chest. "*My* shower."

"But I'm renting this house."

"You can't be renting this house. My grandma owns it."

"Grandma Saffron?" He smiles. "I can't wait to meet her."

My breath hitches and tears well in my eyes. "You can't meet her. You can never meet her. She's gone."

"I'm sorry, Indy."

Warmth fills those gray eyes and he reaches for me. If he touches me, I'll end up naked in the shower with him. The idea has appeal – oh, so much sexy appeal – until I remember how he walked away from me without a backward glance. I step back.

Katy Purry snarls. I tighten my hold but she's a kitty on a mission. She launches from my arms straight at Cash.

He tries to evade her and ends up slipping on the shower floor. He flails his arms to stop from falling, but Katy Purry lands on his chest and tips him over. They slam to the floor of the shower. My kitty swipes her nails at his face. He somehow manages to catch her to hold her away from him.

"Save me! Your kitten is the devil."

I stare at him wriggling on the floor while trying to keep my kitty from clawing him. I wish I was the type of person who could be cold and cruel and get her revenge by allowing my cat to claw him until red welts appear all over his body. But I'm not.

I'm also not the woman who will gawk at his naked body no matter how tempted I am. I throw a towel over him before snatching Kity Purry from his hands.

"Get dressed. We need to talk."

His jaw clenches. Cash hates talking. Explanations? Not if he can help it.

But I'm not accepting no for an answer. If he won't tell me why he's showering in Grandma's house, I'll phone the police and have him removed from the premises.

"You have five minutes before I call the police."

He rolls his eyes. "You won't call the police."

I lean over and hiss in his face. "You don't know me any-more."

Pain flashes in his eyes, but I ignore it. It's his fault he doesn't know me. Not mine.

I whirl around and march toward the hallway.

"And the name is Indigo," I holler over my shoulder.

Cash was the only person to ever use the nickname Indy. But he's no longer special. He'll refer to me as Indigo the way everyone else does. If I allow him to talk to me at all.

Chapter 2

Cash – A rockstar who's wondering why there's no security to save him from the world's meanest cat

Cash

Indy – Indigo – doesn't shut the bathroom door on her way out, and I watch her pert ass bounce up and down as she storms off. Indigo mad is a thing of beauty. Her cheeks darken, storm clouds build in her hazel eyes, and—

Shit. I'm getting hard.

I clear my throat and switch off the water in the shower. I wrap the towel around my waist before hurrying to the bedroom and throwing on some clothes. Water and shampoo drip down my back, but I ignore it. I need to hurry or Indigo may disappear.

She's not mine. She'll never be mine. She's all apple pie and white picket fences. In other words, perfect. I will never be good enough for her.

But knowing she'll never be mine won't stop me from stealing every moment I can with her. Besides, I need to know what she's doing here. Does this house really belong to her grandma? And what happened to Grandma Saffron?

I scan for the devil cat as I hurry down the stairs. When I don't spot the furry monster, I continue on my way but skid to a halt when I notice Indigo on the sofa. Her body shakes as tears stream down her face.

I'm probably the last person in the world she wants to comfort her, but I don't care. I sit next to her and pull her into my arms. I resist the urge to sniff her hair as she cries into my chest. My t-shirt is soaked before she quiets.

I know the second she realizes it's me because she freezes before pushing me away and scurrying to the other end of the sofa. Her eyes are puffy and red rimmed but she's still the most beautiful woman I've ever laid eyes on.

She has more freckles than she used to. I remember tracing every single one with my tongue over and over again before I'd latch onto those perfect bowtie lips while my hands would delve into her curly auburn hair. I wonder if it still smells of strawberries.

I force myself not to drop my gaze to peruse her body. I never fail to get hard when I study her curves and now is not the time to be randy.

"What happened?" I ask.

"Grandma died of c-c-cancer. She… She… She never…" She blows out a breath and composes herself. "She never told me she was sick. She died here alone while I was several states away. I should have been here. She should have told me!"

She bursts into tears again and I surge across the couch, intent on pulling into my arms, but she bats me away.

"What are you doing here?" she demands.

Those hazel eyes flare, and I fist my hands to stop myself from reaching for her again. The woman is temptation wrapped up in a short, curvy package. And I'm past ready to open my gift.

"I'm renting this house."

"No, you aren't."

"Yes, I am."

"No. You can't be. This must be a mistake."

It's not. The band's personal assistant drove us into town after our last stop on the tour and got me settled here last night. Aurora doesn't make mistakes.

"Do you think I broke in here and now I'm squatting?"

She raises her eyebrows. "You do know how to pick a lock."

My cheeks warm. I wasn't exactly a model citizen as a teenager and Indigo was there every step of the way warning me not to throw my life away.

"I didn't pick the lock."

"Fine. You didn't pick the lock. But what are you doing here in this house, in this town? You have a gazillion dollars. You could be anywhere."

"I don't have a gazillion dollars." I don't know what a gazillion dollars is.

She waves my comment away. "Why are you here in Winter Falls?"

"We're recording our new album here."

She rears back. "In Winter Falls? My Winter Falls? The small town that prides itself on being the saviors of the earth?"

I chuckle. "The saviors of the earth?"

She ignores my question and repeats hers. "Why are you here?"

"I told you. *Cash & the Sinners* are recording our newest album here."

Her forehead wrinkles. "Where?"

"*Bertie's Recording Studio.*"

"There's a recording studio in Winter Falls?" I nod. "Wow. A lot has changed in five years since I was last here."

"You haven't been here for five years?" Indigo used to visit Winter Falls every summer with her mom. "Why not?"

"It's a long story."

I open my mouth to ask. I want to know everything that happened in her life since I last saw her eleven years ago but she speaks before I have the chance.

"But why are you here?" She points to the floor. "In this house. My grandma's house."

"I rented it via a rental agent."

I don't mention my assistant handled the arrangements. Guessing by the gazillion dollar comment, Indigo is not impressed with my fame. And she shouldn't be. Fame isn't what it's made out to be.

"Rental agent? There's a rental agent in Winter Falls?"

I chuckle. "I guess a lot has changed in town."

"But when did you arrive? Was Grandma here?"

Hope sparks in her eyes and I hate to dash it. "I got in last night."

"Oh." She scratches her neck. "I still don't understand how you rented this place so quickly after…"

She doesn't need to finish her sentence. I get it.

She clears her throat and stands. "Obviously, the rental agreement is no longer valid."

I stand as well. "What do you mean? Where am I going to stay?"

"Not here. You can't stay here."

"But I need somewhere to live while we record the album." And I'm not abandoning Indigo while she's grieving.

She crosses her arms over her chest and my gaze dips briefly to those breasts I want to feel in my hands once again. I clear my throat. Wrong timing.

"Why is this my problem?" she asks.

"I have a rental agreement."

She waves my comment away. "Stay at the *Inn on Main*."

I frown. Staying at the bed and breakfast in town means coming across strangers constantly. Strangers who won't fail to recognize me. We came to Winter Falls for a bit of quiet, not to be chased by fans.

But I keep my mouth shut. I'm not reminding her of my fame.

"Where's the rest of the band staying?"

"They're sharing two apartments."

"Go stay with them."

Now it's my turn to cross my arms over my chest. "They're staying in two two-bedroom apartments. I'm not sleeping on the couch. My days of couch surfing are over."

"There you go. You're a famous rockstar." Shit. I shouldn't have said anything about couch surfing. "Surely, you have an assistant who can figure this situation out for you."

I don't want to contact my assistant. The band gave her a month off. She deserves it after dealing with us for the past months as we finished our tour.

"What if I stay here?" I suggest.

"Bad idea."

She's not wrong. Being around the temptation of Indigo Scott is a bad idea. I'll never be able to keep my hands off of her, but we can't have a relationship.

She deserves someone steady. Someone who's home every night. Someone who doesn't spend his nights traveling in buses from state to state. Someone who doesn't have women throw their panties at him. Someone who's not me. But I can't leave her alone.

"I'll stay out of your hair. I'll be busy recording anyway."

She bites her bottom lip and I stuff my hands in my pockets before I reach forward to pull her lip free of her teeth. My hands vibrate with the desire to touch her. Yeah, this is a bad idea. But bad ideas are my bread and butter.

Her shoulders deflate and I know I've won.

"Fine. You can stay here, but you'll stay out of my hair. And you need to find other accommodations as soon as possible."

"Why do I need other accommodations?"

"Because I'm selling this house as soon as I can and then I'm leaving."

My heart clenches. Leaving? Indigo's leaving already?

Fuck the album. I'm spending every single second I can with her until she's gone. My memories of her need to last me for a lifetime.

Chapter 3

Temptation – When you really, really want to do something you know you shouldn't but oh boy would it be fun

INDIGO

For a second, I don't know where I am. This isn't my bed. This isn't my bedroom. I sniff. It smells familiar. *Grandma.* I smile before I remember. She isn't here. She never will be again.

Tears threaten but I blink them away. I've cried more over the past few days than I have since…

I slam my fist against the mattress. I am not going there. I'm not going to think about how Cash tore my heart in two and threw the pieces away without a backward glance.

I scowl. I'm doing an awesome job of not going there.

Meow! My cat pounces on me.

"And good morning to you, too, Katy Purry."

Meow!

"I get it. You're hungry. Can I have some coffee first?"

She swipes a paw at my shoulder.

"Guess not."

I throw the blankets off and roll out of bed. My bare feet hit the floor and I yelp.

"Cold. Cold. Cold."

I'm not used to the cold having grown up in San Diego. I spent quite a bit of time in Winter Falls growing up but it was always during the summer. Grandma came to San Diego for Christmas until the 'big fight'.

I find my thick socks and throw a hoodie on over my flannel pajamas. Time for coffee.

I open the bedroom door and Katy Purry rushes out and down the hall.

She snarls before someone growls, "Don't you dare, demon cat."

Cash. I still can't believe he's here. What are the odds of him recording an album in Winter Falls at the same time Grandma died? Is it serendipity? Or just really bad luck? The worst kind of luck. The 'you thought you were over him but you're not' kind of luck.

"I'm warning you, cat."

Cash's grumble reminds me I can't stand in the hallway contemplating my love life forever. I have a will reading to attend this morning. My eyes well with tears but I blink them away. I'm not crying again! Instead, I force my feet to move.

I enter the kitchen but skid to a stop at the vision in front of me. Cash is brandishing a ladle at my kitty while wearing nothing but a pair of boxers.

I ignore Katy Purry. She's harmless. Mostly.

My eyes are glued to Cash's nearly naked form. I got a glimpse of it yesterday but I refused to stare considering I barged into the bathroom and ripped open the shower curtain without his permission.

I'm paying attention now. He certainly didn't have those six-pack abs when we were together. He was lean then, but not muscular. His boxers hang low on his hips giving me a glimpse of hair. Hair, he didn't have back in the day either. A slight push from me and those boxers would fall to the floor to reveal his manhood in all its glory.

I feel liquid gather between my thighs. Before I can rub my legs together to get a bit of relief, Cash glances over at me and smirks.

"Good morning, sleepyhead."

The smirk sets me off. It's the same smirk he uses in all his publicity photos. Who does he think I am? I'm not some rabid fan. I knew him when he was living off leftovers I'd sneak to him from my house.

"Are you having hot flashes?"

He cocks a brow, and butterflies wake in my stomach. Why is cocking a brow so dang sexy?

I ignore those butterflies – they only bring me trouble – and motion to his lack of clothes. "Why else are you strutting around like it's 90 degrees in here when there's snow in the forecast?"

"You know I run hot."

Oh boy, do I ever. When we slept together, I never needed a blanket. Cash could keep me warm. I resist the temptation to fan myself – this is the boy who broke my heart when he threw me away, after all – and scowl instead.

"Don't be a dick."

He chuckles. "Still not swearing?"

"I teach elementary school. Swearing is frowned upon in front of small children with big ears who tend to repeat everything they hear."

He smiles. This time it's not the stupid rockstar smirk. No, this is his real smile. "You did it. You finished your degree and are living your dream."

Not hardly. My dream included Cash as my husband. And maybe two or three little boys with gray eyes scampering around at our feet. But my dream burst into flames at our high school graduation.

"You can't strut around the house half naked."

"Oh, darling, this is not naked."

Wrong thing to say. I know exactly how he's used to being naked with his fans. How he picks a skinny blonde at every venue to take back to his hotel room.

I peer down at my big boobs and wide hips. I don't know what he ever saw in me. Maybe none of it was real to him. Maybe I was a meal ticket he could cash whenever he needed. But it was real to me.

I cross my arms over my chest and give him my best glare. It's been known to cause six-year-old boys to pee their pants. A fact I'm not proud of.

"I am not one of your groupies. And this isn't some penthouse in a hotel. This is my grandmother's home and you will treat me and it with some respect or you can leave."

Those gray eyes I loved to stare into while he moved inside of me flash with pain before he clears his throat and ducks his chin. "Of course. I'm sorry."

"Good. Now, I need some coffee and to feed my cat."

I'm surprised Katy Purry hasn't let her annoyance with the delay of her breakfast be known. Where is she anyway? I scan the room and gasp when I spot her.

"Bad kitty," I murmur as I pull her claws away from Cash's leg. Blood seeps out of the wounds.

"Oh, ship! You're bleeding."

I shove Katy Purry toward him. "Hold her while I get the first aid kit."

"I'm not holding the fur devil."

"She's not the devil."

He motions toward his legs. "I beg to differ."

"She's not used to strangers is all."

"How does she handle your boyfriend?"

"She—" I cut myself off before I tell him there is no boyfriend. "Nice try. And none of your business."

He shrugs. "You can't blame a guy for trying."

Wrong. I most definitely can. And I will.

I glimpse the clock and notice the time. Drat! I'm going to be late.

"I don't have time for this. I have an appointment with a lawyer this morning for the reading of the will."

"I'll feed the fur monster. You go get ready. I know how much you hate to be late."

I do. I really do. Being late makes me break out in hives. Itchy hives I can't help myself from scratching. But still, I ask, "Are you sure?"

"Go. I got this. I'll bring you some coffee."

"But kitty—"

"I can handle a woman with claws."

I ignore the comment. I don't want to know. "Thanks."

I hand him Katy Purry. His nose wrinkles, and she hisses at him.

"You're stuck with me, devil cat."

As much as I'd enjoy watching Katy Purry take him down – and there's no doubt in my mind he'd be on the losing end of a fight between the two – I don't have time. I start toward the stairs but Cash catches my hand.

"Do you want me to go with you?"

To the shower? Yes, please! Cash naked in the shower. Hot and wet as his hands glide over my body until— *Stop it, Indigo!* There will be no imagining Cash naked.

"You are not showering with me."

This is why we shouldn't be staying in the same house. I could barely resist Cash Evans when he was a scrappy teenager trying to survive after his mom died while refusing to go into care. There's no way I can resist Cash the rockstar.

"I meant to the reading of the will."

I need a moment to push thoughts of us together in the shower all soapy and slippery out of my mind.

"Oh."

He doesn't want to shower with me, he wants to go to the reading of the will with me. Do I want him to sit next to me and hold my hand while I listen to the last wishes of the grandma I loved more than my own mother? More than anything.

Which is why it's not happening. His support would mean the world to me. To him, it's just a favor for an old friend.

I sniff. "No, thank you. I'll be fine."

Eventually.

Chapter 4

The Gossip Gals – Five women who think they're the bee's knees

Indigo

I stare in the mirror as I smooth down my skirt. Dang it. My cheeks are still flushed. What was I thinking? Using the time in the shower to think about Cash while touching myself? I'm behind schedule. I hate being late. And, yet, I couldn't help myself.

The man is a drug to me and I would happily jump into addiction with him. But I won't. He doesn't want me.

The thought has the flush on my cheeks disappearing. Cash doesn't want me. Good reminder.

My gaze catches on to the coffee cup on the dresser. The coffee cup Cash brought me while I got ready. This isn't him wanting me, I remind myself. This is him being nice.

And what am I doing thinking about a man when the reading of Grandma's will is this morning? Grandma would say I'm boy crazy. She's not wrong.

The doorbell rings and I hurry to answer it since I sincerely doubt a rockstar would deign to answer the door.

"Hello," I greet the five elderly ladies standing on the porch. "Can I help you?"

"You don't remember us?"

I study the ladies. They appear vaguely familiar.

"Are you friends of my grandma?"

They smile at me.

"You remind me of her," says one.

"She's Saffron when she was thirty without a doubt," says another.

My stomach cramps. I place a hand over it as guilt swamps me. I should have visited Grandma more often. I should know these friends of hers.

Why did I stay away? I visited the first summers after Mom and Grandma had their fight. Why did I let Mom stop me from visiting after that? There's no way Grandma did anything to deserve being abandoned by me.

Nails clickity clack on the hardwood floor before Katy Purry barrels into me. Cash is hot on her heels.

"Sorry, the devil cat got away from me," he says.

I gather my kitty in my arms. "Cash Evans, if you don't stop calling my cat the devil, I won't stop her the next time she thinks your penis is a sausage."

"Has the cat seen Cash's penis?"

"Who cares about the cat? Has Indigo seen his penis?"

"Of course, she has. They were high school sweethearts."

"Recently. Has she seen it recently?"

My face warms. I haven't seen it recently but I sure as heck was imagining it while I was showering.

One of the ladies points to my face. "She has. It's confirmed."

Another lady claps. "This is going to be my favorite project yet."

"Every project is your favorite."

"Good thing we handled the rental situation."

Rental situation? They're responsible for me and Cash being forced to live together? I open my mouth to ask them for an explanation, but Cash throws his arm over my shoulders and speaks before I get the chance.

"Hello, ladies. I'm Cash. And you are?"

I lock my limbs to stop myself from shivering at the sound of his voice. He's using the honey-coated deep sexy voice fans around the world have fallen in love with. I am not immune no matter how much I may wish otherwise.

"We know you're Cash."

"You're Cash from *Cash & the Sinners.*"

Cash's brow wrinkles. "You know who I am?"

"We're old. Not dead."

"You're not the first celebrity to visit Winter Falls."

"We are very proud of Ashlyn and *Bertie's Recording Studio.*"

I clear my throat. "I'm afraid I don't remember your names," I say in a lame attempt to stop them from spiraling further out of control.

"I'm Sage," says the woman standing at the front of the group. She indicates each person in turn. "This is Feather, Petal, Cayenne, and Clove."

"We're the gossip gals," Feather announces.

Cash chuckles and I elbow him. "Be polite."

"What? She said it first."

"It's lovely to meet all of you. Again," I add when they purse their lips at my greeting. "I'm sorry I don't remember you very well."

Sage reaches out to pat my hand but Katy Purry bellows at her. She snags her hand back. "My, my what an interesting cat you have there."

Cash grunts. "She named her Katy Purry." He feigns a shiver. "After a pop star."

I sigh. "Pop music is the second most listened to music genre."

He smirks. "But rock is the first."

"By a smidgeon of a margin."

"How do you know? Did you look up the numbers?"

Of course, I did. He's teased me about my love of pop forever. He acts as if I'm the only person in the world who enjoys music from Katy Perry, Taylor Swift, and Lady Gaga. Obviously, he's wrong.

"I told you this was going to be my favorite project," Petal says.

She mentioned the project before. What's she talking about? "What do you mean? Project?" I ask.

Sage grins. "Never you mind."

Cash barks out a laugh. Since his arm is still around my shoulders, I feel how his body trembles with his laughter. I want to lean into him and enjoy his happiness. Shoot! I am leaning into him.

I step away and his arm drops. And now I feel cold without his warmth surrounding me. Here I thought I was a mess from Grandma passing. Apparently, I'm just plain a mess with a capital M.

I need to get myself out of this situation pronto. Good thing I have the perfect excuse.

"It was lovely meeting you but I need to get going."

Clove waves away my words. "Mr. West will wait."

"How do you know I'm meeting with Mr. West?" Mr. West is the attorney handling Grandma's estate.

Feather giggles. "This is Winter Falls."

Is repeating the name of the town supposed to be an answer? "And?"

"And we're the gossip gals," Sage answers.

This is literally the most confusing conversation I've had and I deal with six-year-olds all day long.

"We're usually wearing matching shirts," Petal says.

Sage frowns. "But someone forgot to buy new gold sparkly fabric paint."

Feather scowls. "I already apologized. No need to beat a dead horse."

"There will be no beating of any animals of any kind," Cayenne says. "We don't believe in violence in Winter Falls."

"She knows," Petal claims. "She practically grew up here."

"Except she hasn't visited in five years," Sage says and all the women focus on me.

My cheeks warm. I open my mouth to defend myself but what defense do I have? Mommy told me not to? I'm a grown woman. I need to own up to my mistakes. I straighten my back but before I have a chance to speak, Cash does.

"You will not give Indigo a hard time this week," he grumbles as he shackles my wrist and hauls me near. Good thing I have Katy Purry in my hands or else I'd melt into him. No melting allowed! "Do I need to remind you she just lost her grandmother?"

Petal sighs. "Favorite project."

Sage nods. "Yes, we've made the right decision."

Cayenne glares at her. "*We* didn't make the decision. Saffron did."

Sage waves away her comment. "But we're the ones who have to carry out her plans."

What in the world are they talking about? Are they all senile? Did they escape from the local senior facility? Do I need to phone the police to escort them back?

Sage wags a finger in my face. "Don't look at us like we're crazy. You'll see." She snaps her fingers. "Gossip gals move out."

"She thinks she's the boss," Feather says with a roll of her eyes.

"She's not," Cayenne agrees as she follows them.

"Bye!" Petal and Clove wave as they join the rest.

I watch until they round the corner and are out of sight.

"What just happened?"

Cash chuckles. "I don't know but they're fun."

I set Katy Purry down and pick up my purse. "I don't have time for fun."

"You used to make time for fun."

His voice rumbles through me until I'm tingling from my fingers to my toes. I ignore the delicious feeling and march to the door.

"I also used to be a teenager who believed in fairy tales." Ugh! Why did I say those words? Why bring up the past? It only causes me pain. "I need to go."

I'm on the porch breathing the sweet air of relief when he catches my hand to stop me. "You certain you don't want me to come with?" When I don't immediately answer, he pushes. "I can cancel today's recording session. It's no problem."

Thanks for the reminder. He's not my Cash. He's a rockstar now.

"I'll be fine."

I yank my hand away from him and flee before I can change my mind. Before I forget how he doesn't want me. How he threw me away.

Chapter 5

Band – Similar to a family except when you tease one, they might try to kill you

CASH

As I watch Indigo walk away from me, I debate ignoring her wishes and accompanying her to the meeting with the lawyer, but I know better. She'd slam the door in my face with a smirk on hers.

The devil cat pushes against my legs. I catch her before she can escape. I don't care if she's allowed outside, I'm not letting her loose to terrorize the neighborhood dogs.

My phone buzzes. I don't bother to read the message. I know I'm late. But, unlike Indigo, I don't give a shit.

Thirty minutes later I stroll into the recording studio. I'm surprised by how professional the place appears. *Rotten Lies* recorded their last album here and they recommended the studio but I honestly didn't believe it would be this nice.

The main reason the band agreed to record here is because of the anonymity. We're exhausted from fans and groupies and need a bit of down time.

Don't get me wrong. I know how lucky we are to have fans and groupies, but sometimes we need a break from it all.

The other band members are already in the studio. I wave to the producer and studio engineer as I pass them in the sound room before joining the band.

"Nice digs," I greet.

"Easy for you to say," Fender grumbles. "You didn't have to listen to Gibson snore all night."

Fender is the bassist for *Cash & the Sinners*. He's also a total grump.

Gibson throws a pick at him. "I don't snore."

I snort. Gibson totally snores. I've spent more nights than I can count wearing earplugs on the tour bus to drown out the horse-like sounds he makes when he's sleeping.

"The women never complain." He wiggles his eyebrows. In addition to being our rhythm guitarist, Gibson is a charmer. He can talk a woman out of her panties in two seconds flat. It's true. We've timed him.

"I slept fine," Dylan says before an argument between Gibson and Jett can break out over who is the bigger womanizer. As if being a womanizer is something to be proud of.

Jett laughs. "Probably because I slept elsewhere."

I cross my arms over my chest and glare at him. I have no intention of listening to Jett's exploits. Jett is our drummer and never met a dare or a woman he didn't like. Someday it's going to get him in trouble. Lord help us all when it happens.

"Enough," I growl. "We're here to record an album not sleep with every available woman over eighteen in town."

Gibson smirks. "The age of consent in Colorado is seventeen."

I cock an eyebrow. "But at what age does a dad stop aiming a shotgun at men who corrupt his daughter?"

Dylan bursts out laughing. "You're the only one who experienced a dad with a shotgun."

I glare at him. He's my best friend and the best damn lead guitarist I could ask for but he knows better than to bring up my past with Indigo.

Except… maybe Indigo isn't my past. Maybe she can be my future. I shake my head. No way. She deserves better than me.

"Are we going to record an album or are we going to sit around all day and gossip like a bunch of old ladies?"

Jett raises his hand. "I vote for gossiping."

Of course, he does. He wants to tell us all about his night. The man thinks the phrase 'don't kiss and tell' should be 'kiss and tell'. If I hear one more description of a woman's tramp stamp, I'm going to shove his sticks up his ass.

The mic squeaks before Stan, our producer, chimes in, "We don't have this studio forever."

Fender gives him the middle finger. Stan ignores him since the middle finger is Fender's favorite and he doesn't hesitate to use it.

"You heard the man." I nod toward the equipment. "Let's make some music."

"I thought we were on a break," Fender grumps.

"You can be on a break once you finish this album," Stan announces.

"Fender's not wrong," Dylan says. "We finished our last tour two days ago. We were promised a break after the tour was extended."

Jett twirls his sticks in the air. "I don't need a break."

"Have you slept?"

"Who needs sleep?" He winks.

I groan. Sex is a drug to Jett. He'll be on a high for a few hours before he crashes. Hard. And we'll pay the price.

Gibson opens his guitar case and screams. "Who did this? Where is my guitar? I'm going to kill you, Jett."

He raises a miniature pink guitar in the air and pounces toward Jett who jumps from his stool and flees the studio.

"You can't catch me. I'm the gingerbread man," Jett sings as Gibson chases him around the studio.

I groan and collapse on the sofa.

"At least, our label rented out the entire studio for us," Dylan says as he sits down next to me.

"Break time," Fender declares as he opens a container. The smell of pancakes and sausage wafts out and my stomach grumbles.

"Smells good."

Good? I'm practically drooling. It smells great. When we're on tour, I try to eat healthy. Putting on a two-hour show every night is a workout. It requires stamina. Unfortunately, eating junk food messes with my stamina.

Fender cradles the container to his chest. "Mine."

I don't care. I'm starving. And ready to break my diet for some real food.

When we got in last night, the small town was already asleep despite it being early. The bar was open, but it doesn't serve food. I tried to order food online but none of the usual apps deliver to Winter Falls.

I raided the kitchen at Indigo's grandma's house but the only food in there was milk and goat's cheese. Since goat's cheese is nearly as disgusting as goat's milk, I went to bed hungry. I debated stealing some of Indigo's food this morning but I got distracted by five old ladies and a demon cat.

I snatch the container from Fender.

"Typical," he growls at me before reaching down and picking up an identical container.

I dig into the pancakes. Dylan snags a sausage link and I snap my teeth at him.

"Don't hurt the fingers."

"Don't steal my food," I say with my mouth full of pancake and syrup.

"You stole it from Fender."

"But he knew I would, so it doesn't count."

"If I find your guitar, will you stop chasing Jett?" Rob, the studio engineer, asks.

I don't hear Gibson's response but I do hear Rob yelp. "Hey! It was just a question."

Stan enters the studio. "If I have to handle those two, I won't be nice."

In other words, I need to handle this. I pass my half-finished breakfast to Dylan, who doesn't hesitate to dig in, and stand.

"I am not in the mood for this today."

Dylan chuckles. "When are you in the mood to deal with Twiddle Dee and Twiddle Dum?"

I don't bother responding. He knows how fed up I get with Gibson and Jett's fooling around. The only things those two are serious about are Gibson's guitars and Jett's sticks. Considering Jett's messing with Gibson's guitars, this won't be pretty.

I stomp out of the studio through the control room. Gibson and Jett are running circles through the rest of the building where there are two other studios.

I stick my fingers in my mouth and whistle. They freeze.

"It's his fault," Gibson accuses.

"We're only having fun," Jett claims.

"Fun?" Gibson's nostrils flare. "You messed with one of my guitars."

Jett rolls his eyes. "I would never mess with your guitar. I'm messing with you."

"Are you done now?" I ask before they can continue this bullshit conversation. "We have a record to make."

Jett waits until Gibson heads toward me before sticking his tongue out at his back and following.

"Herding cats would be easier," I grumble as I follow them back into the studio.

Although, I imagine trying to herd Katy Purry and another cat into a room would not be easier. I'm not joking when I say Indigo's cat is the devil. It's beady little eyes give it away. I'm going to lock my door tonight to stop the little fur monster from invading while I sleep.

Indigo, on the other hand, is welcome to invade whenever she wants. My cock perks up as memories of all the times I snuck into her bedroom when we were teenagers flit through my mind.

Too bad Indigo's not the kind of girl you can use for a bit of fun – she's the engagement ring and wedding dress kind of girl – because Indigo in bed without her clothes on is synonymous with fun.

Chapter 6

Surprise – When your grandmother meddles in your life from beyond the grave

INDIGO

"You must be Indigo," a man says the moment I enter the office inside the courthouse on Main Street.

"Mr. West?"

He shakes my hand before shutting the door. "It's impossible to keep the gossip under control but I do try." He ushers me toward a chair in front of his desk.

"I met a few women who said they were the gossip gals this morning."

He chuckles as he sits in his desk chair. "Those women."

I guess he knows who they are. "They kept on referring to a project but they wouldn't explain. Do you know what they meant?"

"They're harmless."

I cock a brow. "Harmless?"

"They enjoy matchmaking and placing bets about the couples they match. It's completely harmless."

Hold on. They mentioned a project after they 'handled the rental agreement'. Surely, they don't intend to match me with Cash. No way. No how. No—

Why am I worrying about this? I don't live in Winter Falls.

"Well, they won't be matchmaking me since I won't be in town long."

"Ah, yes, Saffron's estate."

The reason I'm in his office. I need to handle Grandma's estate. *Grandma's estate.* I hate those words since they mean Grandma's gone. I swallow the giant sized lump in my throat.

He shuffles some papers on his desk. "Shall we get to it?"

I nod since I can't get any words to come out.

"Do you want me to read her will word for word or get straight to the important stuff?"

I don't want to be here any longer than necessary.

"Important stuff," I squeak out.

"Saffron left all of her worldly possessions to you. Her house, her stocks and bonds, and any cash remaining in her bank account."

"Nothing for her daughter? My mom?"

His face softens. "I'm sorry. Saffron made her wishes quite clear. I believe her exact words were 'my close-minded daughter will get nothing'."

Sounds like Grandma.

"Do you know what the argument between Grandma and my mom was about?"

I've been begging both of them to tell me for years but to no avail. Grandma was as stubborn as a donkey and Mom isn't much better.

"As far as I know, Saffron didn't tell anyone what happened."

My shoulders slump. I'll never learn the truth now. Mom sure isn't talking. When I phoned her to inform her of Grandma's death, she said I was in charge of handling Grandma's affairs and hung up. I was beyond shocked. My mom and I have never gotten along – not in the way Grandma and I do… did – but she's never hung up on me before.

At some point, Mom and I need to talk and iron our stuff out. But first, Grandma's will.

"Grandma had stocks and bonds?"

"I assume you're aware she sold her bookstore, *Fall Into A Good Book,* to my eldest daughter a few years ago."

"Yes." I knew she sold the bookstore, but I didn't know to whom.

"Aspen paid cash for the business and your grandmother invested the money in stocks and bonds." He smiles. "She's actually done quite well for herself."

"Grandma didn't seem the type of person to invest in the stock market."

"She invested in green energy companies."

Ah. Now it makes sense. Grandma was one of the original founders of Winter Falls. Although the town began as a hippie commune, the focus quickly changed from peace and free love to all things environmental.

"Okay," I eventually say as I don't know what else there is to say.

He raises an eyebrow. "Don't you want to know how much her investments are worth?"

I don't really care. I don't want Grandma's money. I want her. I want her to wrap her arms around me in one of her tight hugs I worry will break my ribs. I want her to swat my hand away when I try to steal a piece of pie before dinner. I even want her to ask me one of her thousand embarrassing questions about my sex life.

"The current estimated value of all of Saffron's stocks and bonds is slightly over five hundred thousand dollars."

My jaw drops open. I must be hearing things. He did not say Grandma's investments are worth half a million dollars. No way. No how.

"E-e-excuse me?"

He chuckles. "Five hundred and fifty thousand dollars to be exact."

Holy cow. I had no idea. I never discussed money with Grandma. I cared more about hearing how she discovered a new apple pie recipe, or how her rose bush was doing, or what mystery book she was reading.

"And she left it to me?"

"She has."

"Not to some environmental charity?"

"It's all yours. As soon as the paperwork is filed."

Grandma was wealthy. How did I never know? Never mind. I'll think about this later. I have more pressing issues such as cleaning out her house and getting it ready to sell. And kicking out the tenant who's currently living in the place.

"About the house." Mr. West is an attorney. Surely, he'll know how I can get rid of Cash.

"Ah, yes, the house. There's a stipulation to your inheritance."

"A stipulation? What kind of stipulation?"

"The house is yours provided you live in it for a year."

"Live in Grandma's house?" My brow furrows in confusion. "But I don't live in Winter Falls. I live in San Diego. My life is there. My job, my apartment, my family. I can't uproot myself to live in Winter Falls for a year because Grandma says so."

"Saffron did set aside an allowance for you for living expenses for the year." He chuckles. "Assuming you don't want to cash in the stocks and bonds."

"What am I supposed to do? Be a lady of leisure for a year?" No way. I can't do nothing for a year. I'll go crazy.

"You could teach at the local school."

I narrow my eyes on him. "How do you know I'm a teacher?"

"Saffron was very proud of you." Of course. He was friends with Grandma. Naturally, she told him what I do for a living.

Before I can apologize for jumping down his throat, he continues, "My wife happens to be the principal of the local school. She also happened to mention she has a vacancy for an elementary school teacher this morning."

"She happened to mention?"

He shrugs. "I can't keep secrets from my wife. She knew I was meeting with you this morning."

"And she knew the stipulations of the will," I finish.

"Yes."

"What if I don't want to stay here? What if I want to go home?"

"The house will be torn down."

"Torn down?" I clasp my chest. "But it's the home Grandpa built for her."

"Not to mention the people of Winter Falls will have an absolute shit fit if a perfectly good home were demolished."

My eyes widen. I hadn't thought of the town's reaction.

"Excuse my language."

I wave away his apology. I don't care about his language. I care how Grandma is manipulating me from the grave.

"Can't I rent the house out for a year and then sell it?"

"I'm afraid there are no loopholes. You can't rent the house. You can't let it sit empty. You absolutely must live in the house in Winter Falls for one year to inherit or the house will be torn down."

"She thought of everything," I grumble.

"I may have helped." He winks.

I slump in my chair. What am I supposed to do? Staying in Winter Falls wasn't part of the plan. The plan was to clear out Grandma's house and sell it. And I need to arrange a funeral.

A funeral. My stomach bottoms out at the idea of saying a final goodbye to Grandmother. I inhale a deep breath before asking, "Did Grandma have any last wishes about her funeral?"

Mr. West hands me an envelope. "I believe you'll find nearly everything is already arranged or planned."

I clutch the envelope to my chest. I should have known Grandma would plan her own funeral. She did prefer things done her way.

"Thank you." I stand. "I guess I'll be going."

"Are you going to stay in Winter Falls?"

I want to say no. I want to run as far as I can from Winter Falls until the pain in my chest subsides. Until I forget my precious grandmother won't be ringing me every Saturday morning anymore.

"I don't know."

It's the truth. I don't know. With the stocks and bonds Grandma left me, I don't need the money from the sale of the house. But the thought of her home being demolished makes my stomach feel the same way I do after I eat a bag of peanut M&Ms – nauseous.

"You're young. A year is not forever."

True. A year isn't forever. But living in Winter Falls was never part of my plans.

"I know but this isn't part of my life plan."

He studies me. "Maybe it's time to change your life plan. A bit of spontaneity can spice things up."

Spontaneity? He can keep it. He didn't wake up to a rockstar strutting around his kitchen in his boxer shorts. Speaking of rockstars.

"Do you know anything about Saffron renting out her house?"

He clears his throat. What he doesn't do is answer, which is an answer in and of itself. He knows, but he's not talking.

"Can I tear up the rental agreement since Grandma's gone?"

He frowns. "I'm afraid not."

Am I stuck living with Cash in my house? Not if I don't live here.

"Leaving Winter Falls is becoming more and more appealing by the minute."

"Please stay. Saffron wouldn't have made the stipulation without a reason."

But what reason? Why did she want me to stay in Winter Falls? Did she know Cash would rent the house? And why didn't she tell me any of this before?

"I will." I doubt I'll think of anything else until I make up my mind.

There goes my plan to leave Winter Falls as quick as I can. Thanks, Grandma. Supreme Meddler of the Universe.

Chapter 7

Secret – Won't remain unknown for long in Winter Falls

Cash

"Stop!" I throw my mic on the floor. "This isn't working."

"No shit," Dylan grumbles.

I throw him a glare before addressing the rest of the band, "Anyone else want to complain about my lyrics?"

Fender, Gibson, and Jett hold up their hands. They know better than to mess with me when I'm in a 'mood' as they say.

"Why don't you go for a walk?" Dylan suggests.

A walk? I don't want to go for a fucking walk. I want to nail these lyrics. What the hell was I thinking writing a song about the girl I lost? Now I can't get pictures of Indigo out of my mind. Inconvenient since I'm currently sharing a house with the woman.

But not a bed. Which is what I really what to share with her. Hot sweaty nights, our naked bodies entwined, as I sink into her. My cock perks up at the idea. I tell him to settle down. My band mates would tease me until we're too old to get hard-ons if I got hard in front of them.

"I have the number for the woman I nailed last night. Let me send it to you." Jett digs out his phone before I can stop him.

What is he thinking? He knows I don't share women. And, despite the rumors, I don't pick up a new woman every night after a concert.

Have I fucked fans of the band? Of course, I have. I'm not a saint. But I stay away from women who remind me of Indigo. I stick to lanky blondes.

Not women with curves I enjoy digging my fingers into as I— I shove those thoughts away and rub a hand down my face. "A walk sounds nice."

"Nice?" Dylan chuckles. "Since when do you use the word nice?"

I ignore him. He enjoys pushing my buttons. Usually, I push back. But if I push back now, he'll figure out why I'm in a mood. I'm not ready for the band to discover Indigo's in town. I want her all for myself for a while.

I stand from the stool I've been sitting on for hours and stretch my back. "Anyone want to join me?"

Fender, Gibson, and Jett glance away. I guess I've been more than a bit of an asshole today. I should probably apologize. Ask me if I'm going to.

Dylan sighs as he stands. "I'll go with you. Don't want you getting into a fistfight with the locals."

I scowl. "One time. One time I got into a fight. And it wasn't my fault."

"Your fist just happened to ram itself into the reporter's face?"

"He claimed I'm a womanizer."

I know I sound crazy, but I can't stand it when anyone accuses me of being a man whore. Yes, I have issues. But who doesn't?

"We'll pack up," Gibson volunteers as Dylan and I make our way out of the recording booth.

"Thanks." There. I'm not a complete asshole. I thanked my band for doing their jobs. I deserve a pat on the back.

We step outside and I shiver. I may run hot, but Colorado is freezing compared to our last tour stops in Florida and Texas.

I'm also underdressed in a long-sleeved t-shirt, but there's no way I'm wearing a bulky jacket and missing the chance to watch Indigo's eyes flame as her gaze roves over my chest.

"You want to grab a beer?"

I stuff my hands in my pockets and turn away from *Naked Falls Brewing*. I do not want to grab a beer at the brewery. Not considering who owns the place.

"Nope."

"You need to speak to Stan. He promised us time off after the tour finished. Instead, we're in the recording studio working on our next album. We need a break."

I ignore Dylan. I can hardly admit I'm the reason we're in Winter Falls working on our album. I didn't know Indigo would be here, but there are other people here. People I've been working up my courage to meet for years.

"I'm serious, Cash. Gibson and Jett need a break before they end up causing trouble."

I snort. "Because they haven't caused any trouble in the past?"

"I'm not talking about fan girls going into a rage when Gibson kicks them out of his bed or when Jett decides to go parachuting an hour before we need to be on stage and ends up in the emergency room because he broke his leg. I'm talking about actual real trouble. The kind lawyers and PR firms can't get them out of."

"Do you not get tired?"

His brow wrinkles. "Do you not remember the time I fell asleep in the closet with my pants around my ankles?"

I chuckle. "Your girl was pissed."

"Didn't stop her from trying to suck me off while I slept."

"I don't mean exhausted and falling asleep."

"What did you mean?"

I blow out a breath. "Don't you get tired of being the referee? Of being the peacemaker?"

He shrugs. "It's who I am."

I envy how sure he is of who he is and of his place in the world. I thought I was sure of who I am, but then I discovered the truth. And have been ignoring it ever since.

We continue along Main Street until a girl barrels into me. I try to sidestep her but she wraps her arms around my legs and holds on tight.

"Are you my uncle?"

Uncle? My heart skips a beat as I study the little blonde girl in front of me. Is she related to me? Is she one of the people I came to Winter Falls to meet? "Excuse me?"

Her nose wrinkles as she stares at me. "You look like my uncles. I have five." She holds up her hand and counts them off. "Riley, Brody, Miller, Elder, and Peace."

Five? If she has five uncles, there are six brothers. I thought there were five. I know all of the names except Peace. Who's Peace?

A woman rushes up to us. "I'm sorry. She got away from me. I hope she's not bothering you."

"I'm not bothering them. This is my uncle," the little girl declares loud enough for people passing on the street to notice.

The woman looks up at me and I can tell the moment she recognizes who we are. Her eyes widen and excitement sparks. To her credit, she doesn't remark on it.

She smiles down at the little girl. "This man is not your uncle."

"But he looks exactly like Uncle Riley and Uncle Brody. They're twins and they're my uncles," she explains to me.

"Sorry, kiddo. I don't know them." It's not a lie. I know *of* them, but I don't know them.

A man saunters up to us. "I hope you're not bothering these men, Skye."

She huffs. "Of course not, Daddy."

He ruffles her hair before looking my way. His eyes spark with recognition. And this recognition isn't because *Cash & the Sinners* is an internationally recognized band. No, he knows exactly who I am. Fuck. My time's up.

"Let's go, Skye. I'm sure we'll be seeing him again." His gaze bores into me as he speaks. Yep. He recognizes me. I wonder which brother he is.

I watch them saunter down the sidewalk. The father glances back one more time before yanking his phone out of his pocket.

He's probably messaging all of his brothers. All six of them. Seven if you count me.

"Ah," Dylan says once they're out of hearing range. "It all makes sense now. I thought you were being an asshole because of Indigo."

Indigo's one reason, but she's not the sole reason. Not this time.

"But it's not about Indigo. You're still hung up on her, but you didn't insist we record our album in this small town in Colorado because of her."

Shit. He's not supposed to know I'm the one behind us being in Winter Falls. I thought he bought Stan's lie when he claimed he found this recording studio.

"This is all about your dad."

There's no sense denying it. Dylan's known me since we formed the band in middle school. He knows I found my biological dad and his family years ago.

"Yeah."

"What are you going to do?"

"I don't know."

He points to the little girl and her dad. "I don't think you have a choice any longer."

Maybe. Maybe not. I've been running away from the truth for years. I can run a little longer.

Chapter 8

Temptation – Cash Evans. He breathes and I'm tempted.

Indigo

I stare at the papers in front of me. There must be some kind of loophole in Grandma's will. A loophole to allow me to sell the house without living in it for a year. There has to be.

The front door opens and Cash strolls in like he owns the place. He's always been sure of himself and his right to be where he is. Even when we were in high school and I knew it was a lie, he had swagger.

"Honey, I'm home," he says when he notices me.

I narrow my eyes on him. This isn't his home. It's not mine either. But it will be for the next twelve months unless I want the house to be torn down.

Torn down? I can't believe Grandma. She knows I would never let this house she loved be destroyed. She also knows I have a life in San Diego. How could she do this to me?

I drop my head to the table with a groan.

"What's wrong?" Cash massages my neck and I bite my tongue to stop my moan.

Good gracious his hands feel good. I love the touch of his calloused fingers on my skin. I close my eyes and allow myself to enjoy it. Just for a moment. Any second now I'm going to tell him to stop. To get his hands off me.

"Indigo, what's going on?" His breath wafts over my neck. I couldn't stop the shiver from coursing through my body now if I wanted to.

He kneels next to me and uses a finger on my chin to lift my head from the table. "What happened? Is it Grandma Saffron?"

I snort. "Ding. Ding. Ding."

He cradles my face. "I'm sorry you lost her."

"I'm sorry you never met her. She would have loved you. She would have shown you off to all her friends. Before asking you to pose naked for her book club."

He chuckles. "Your grandmother sounds awesome."

I inhale a deep breath. "Except she's trying to control my life from the grave."

He kisses my nose before releasing me and sitting next to me. "Explain."

I motion toward the papers. "I went to the reading of the will today." He nods. "Grandma left me everything including this house. But there are 'stipulations'."

He chuckles at my use of air quotes. "What kind of stipulations?"

"I have to live in this house for a year. If I don't, it'll be torn down."

His brow wrinkles. "Torn down? It's a perfectly good house."

"I know!" I throw my arms in the air. "This is her way of manipulating me."

"But why would she want you to live here for a year? What's her angle?"

"Grandma was a sweetheart. She didn't have angles." I thought.

"I beg to differ." He motions toward the papers.

"Whatever," I mumble. I don't want to discuss my grandma and her angles. I need to figure out how to get out of this mess.

"What are you going to do?"

"I don't know. I have a job back home. Family. Friends. A life."

"It's only a year. Those things will still be waiting for you when you get back."

I narrow my eyes on him. "Easy for you to say. You're a rockstar who spends more time in hotel rooms than your home."

His eyes flash with pain. Shoot. I'm being nasty. "Ignore me. I'm a witch."

"You're not a witch. You're upset about your grandma. It's normal."

Ugh! He needs to stop being nice. Stop reminding me of the Cash I fell in love with. He needs to be Cash the rockstar. The man who crooks his finger and women throw their clothes at him. The man I don't know.

"But what would I do for a year here in Winter Falls? I don't have any friends here."

"What about the kids you played with when you visited in the summer?"

"Stop being reasonable."

"Do you want me to be an ass?"

"No," I pout.

"If I recall correctly, you like my ass. More than like my ass."

My cheeks warm as memories of digging my fingers into his rear while he moved inside of me assault me. I loved to arch my back and rub my nipples against his chest and— *Not the time, Indigo. Not the time*. I clear my throat.

"Stop trying to distract me. I need to figure out what to do."

"Indigo, you already made up your mind."

I narrow my eyes and throw daggers at him. Because he's right and I hate it. I hate how he knows me even after all these years. "You don't know I've made up my mind."

"I do. I know you."

How dare he claim to know me? I don't care if it's true. I jump to my feet. "You don't know me. You *knew* me. Not the same thing."

He prowls toward me and I retreat until my back is against the wall. I hold up a hand. "Stop."

To my surprise, he halts.

"Assuming you're correct." He smirks and I snarl. "Assuming I have made up my mind to stay, what about you?"

"What about me?"

"You can't stay here," I claim despite knowing I can't cancel his rental agreement.

"Why not?"

"Because I'll poison your coffee. And not in one go. It'll be a little bit every day to make you feel sicker and sicker until you finally keel over dead."

He laughs. "And here I was worried about demon cat." He scans the room. "Where is the demon anyway?"

"She's outside exploring."

"The poor wildlife. They won't know what hit them."

I cross my arms over my chest. "My cat is not a demon and she doesn't kill other animals." He cocks a brow. "Much."

He runs a hand through his hair and I watch as his bicep muscles bunch with the movement. I want to touch those muscles. Explore them with my hands and mouth.

This is why he can't stay. When he's around all I can think about is stripping him out of his clothes and having my wicked way with him.

But I won't. He doesn't want me. He made his wishes perfectly clear when he dumped me on graduation day all those years ago without an explanation.

"Why'd you leave?"

"I told you. I was at the recording studio all day."

I fist my hands on my hips. His gaze dips to my hips and he bites his bottom lip. I remember how it feels when he bites my lip.

Knock it off! I will not sleep with my ex. It's the first rule with regard to exes – never sleep with one. Never. No matter the temptation. Hands off!

"Not what I was talking about and you know it."

He shoves his hands in his pockets. "You know why. I'm not good enough for you."

"I call bull! I was good enough to sleep with but not good enough to keep."

"It's the truth."

"This is why you can't stay here. You're a big, fat liar. You used me and threw me away. I am done with this conversation."

Before I have a chance to stomp away, Cash is on me. He slams his hands against the wall near my head to cage me in.

"I am not a liar," he growls.

"You used me."

I inhale a deep breath and my breasts graze his chest. Desire sparks in his eyes. I remember how this ended when we were teenagers. With us sweaty, naked, and completely sated. I've never experienced that feeling with another man.

Don't misunderstand me. I haven't been a nun in the past eleven years but no man has ever made me feel the way Cash can. I always end up comparing all men to him. Which is why I'm single most of the time.

I lick my lips and his gaze dips to follow the movement.

"I never used you," he whispers. "I loved you."

"I—" I don't get a chance to finish my thought before his lips are on mine.

I expect them to be cold and harsh with anger but they're as soft as I remember. I sigh and he doesn't hesitate to shove his tongue in my mouth. His taste of coffee, musk, and something unique to Cash hits me and I'm lost. My resistance crumbles.

I grasp the belt loops on his jeans and yank him to me. And now I'm surrounded by all things Cash. His smell, his feel, his taste. I want it all. I want to drown in it.

He presses his hardness against my stomach and warmth pools between my legs. I ground myself against him and he moans before hitching my leg over his hip. I can feel his hard length exactly where I want it.

Except with less clothes. Yes. Less clothes. Good idea. I snap the button on his jeans open but before I can delve in to feel him, the back door rattles.

Meow!

I jerk my lips from Cash's to check on my kitty. I groan at the scene. Katy Purry brought me a present. The bloody, mangled kind.

Cash chuckles and my brain comes back online. What am I doing? I'm about to dry hump my ex in the living room in front of my cat.

I shove his chest but he doesn't budge. "This was a mistake."

"This was not a mistake. You and I together is never a mistake."

"Really? Which is why you left me to become a rockstar?"

"I didn't leave you to become a rockstar."

I sniff. "Sure, you didn't."

"I didn't." He reaches forward to touch me but I slap his hands away.

"Out of my way. I need to deal with Katy Purry."

He steps away and shivers. "Told you she's a devil cat."

"She's not the devil," I grumble as I march to the door and open it. Katy Purry picks up the dead mole, but I stop her. "You are not bringing dead animals into the house."

"Devil cat."

I ignore him. I have a feeling I'm going to be ignoring him a whole lot in the future. Because I can't have sex with him. I can't. If I do, my heart, which doesn't understand reason whatsoever, will latch onto him without a second thought.

Falling in love with Cash again is a heartbreak ready to happen.

Chapter 9

Trick – To force people to do what you want them to do in order to win a bet

Cash

I prowl around my room. I want to invade Indigo's bedroom and finish what we started before the crazy cat interrupted us. But I know she wouldn't welcome my touch. She had a moment of weakness and I exploited it like the asshole I am.

Enough of this bullshit contemplation. I need to get the hell out of here.

I manage to escape the house without being attacked by the demon cat. I don't know what Indigo sees in the thing. Those beady eyes? Whenever she looks at me, I swear she's contemplating how many ways she can kill me.

Indigo probably rescued the cat because everyone else knew better than to adopt a demon and her soft heart wouldn't let the little demon be put down.

I walk in the opposite direction of Main Street. Running into one small girl who claims I'm her uncle is enough for one day.

A man across the street waves at me. I wave back but freeze when I notice he's not wearing any pants. And it's freezing out.

I hurry to him. “Are you okay, sir?”

“Sir? Who you calling sir? Name’s Forest.”

“Hello, Forest. Are you okay?”

“Why wouldn’t I be okay?” He glances down at his dogs. Hold on. Those aren’t dogs. They’re squirrels. On leashes. Forest is definitely not okay.

“Do you know where you live?”

“Why wouldn’t I know where I live? Are you okay, son? Has playing rock music rotted your brain?”

Playing rock music? Does he know who I am?

“Um…”

The group of elderly ladies who stopped by the house the other day bustle toward us.

“Hello, Cash,” Sage greets. “I see you’ve met Forest, our local pet store owner.”

Forest scowls. “You don’t own pets.”

And yet his squirrels are on leashes. He must notice me looking because he answers my unspoken question, “I have to use leashes. Aspen threw a fit when Chip climbed one of her bookshelves. It wasn’t his fault. Her dog attacked him.”

“Your squirrel is named Chip?”

“He’s not a squirrel. He’s a chipmunk. This is Chip and this is Dale.”

I chuckle. Forest is off his rocker, but he’s amusing.

“I thought we agreed you would wear pants when walking your pets during the daytime,” Sage says.

"We agreed to no such thing," he grumbles. "I'm not going to wear pants if I don't want to," he declares before marching off with his chipmunks following him.

I blink. Maybe I'm hallucinating. Except I'm not the band member who experiments with drugs. I don't go near the stuff. I barely drink considering how my mom died.

Which means I really did meet a man not wearing pants out walking his chipmunks.

"Do we need to make sure he gets home all right?"

"He's fine." Feather laces her arm through mine. "What are you doing out at this time of night?"

Night? It's barely seven. Seven is practically noon to me considering we don't usually step onto the stage at one of our concerts before nine.

"Have you had dinner yet?" Clove asks.

My stomach growls in response.

Feather whirls me around and prods me toward Main Street. "You should have dinner at Moon's diner. It's meatloaf night. You can thank me later."

When I don't move, Cayenne pats me on the ass. I'm used to strange women touching my ass, but they're not usually old enough to be my grandmother.

"Go," she urges. "Her meatloaf special tends to sell out."

I shrug. I might as well. Eating at the diner is as good of an excuse as any to avoid staying in a house with Indigo where I'm not allowed to touch her, to kiss her, to strip her naked. I shut down those thoughts before I embarrass myself and wave to the gossip gals.

When I reach Main Street, I realize I didn't ask for directions. I search the area until I notice the sign for *Moon's Diner* sandwiched between a grocery store and a bookstore.

The bell over the door rings as I step inside. A woman hurries toward me.

"Finally." She grabs my hand and drags me to a booth next to the window. "I couldn't save this table for much longer. And I'm running out of meatloaf."

"Boo!" someone shouts.

She plants her hands on her hips. "It's not my fault someone decided to eat four servings."

"He always eats four servings!" he shouts back.

"He's my boyfriend. He can eat as much as he wants," she shouts before turning to me. "I'm Moon. I own this place."

"Nice to meet you."

"What do you want to drink? I know you rockstar types probably mainline vodka but I don't have a liquor license."

I hold up a hand. "I don't drink anything stronger than beer."

"How about a lemonade? I make it myself." She dashes away before I have a chance to respond. I guess I'm having lemonade.

The door opens to the diner and Indigo steps inside. I wave her over and she scowls before marching to me.

"This is why the gossip gals told me I had to try the meatloaf today."

I chuckle. "They told me the same thing."

"Meanwhile, the refrigerator at Grandma's house is stuffed full of dishes the neighbors have been bringing over all day. What were they thinking?"

I peer around the diner. Everyone in the place is focused on us and they're not bothering to hide it.

I lean close to whisper, "I think they're trying to set us up."

"What did you say? I couldn't hear you," someone shouts.

"He said he thinks the gossip gals are trying to set them up," the person in the booth behind us answers.

The place erupts into laughter. Moon arrives with two glasses of lemonade. She smiles at Indigo. "Nice to see you made it."

"Did I have a choice?" Indigo mutters.

Moon barks out her laugh. "Enjoy the ride."

"What ride?" Indigo asks but Moon's already gone. "Who's she?"

I shrug. "All I know is her name is Moon."

Before Indigo can ask any more questions, Moon returns and plops two servings of meatloaf down on the table. "You're welcome."

"Hey! I haven't gotten my food yet and I arrived here before them," the person in the booth behind us complains.

"You'll get your food when it's ready, Sirius," Moon tells him before marching off again.

Indigo moans and I forget all about all the people in the diner watching our every move. I want to hear her moan when my hands are on her naked skin. When she's moaning because she can't contain the pleasure I'm giving her. My cock twitches at the thought.

"This is really good." She frowns at me. "Why aren't you eating?"

I tell my cock to calm the hell down and pick up my fork to dig in. I nearly groan at the taste. This is fabulous. Hands down the best meatloaf I've eaten in my life. Which isn't saying much. My mom wasn't much of a cook and I haven't enjoyed a homemade meal in over a decade.

Conversation is forgotten as we eat our dinners. When I finish, I drop the fork on the plate and lean back to rub my belly.

"Best meatloaf I've ever tasted," I declare.

Indigo giggles. "No kidding. I thought you were going to lick the plate."

I stick my tongue at her. "I was hungry for some comfort food. I eat healthy on tour."

Moon arrives and picks up our plates. "By the way, I'm married to one of the brothers. They know where you're staying and your time's up. Don't say I didn't warn you."

Indigo gapes after her. "What's she talking about?"

"Never mind."

Pain flashes in her eyes. "I don't know why I bothered to ask. You haven't told the truth since our high school graduation."

Crap. I don't want to hurt her but I'm not ready to talk about how I found my dad and discovered my half-brothers live in Winter Falls.

She stands and my chest tightens. I don't want her to walk away mad at me. I shackle her wrist before she can retreat. "Don't go."

"Why should I stay?"

I scan the diner. No one bothers to pretend they aren't following every word of our conversation. "Not here. Let's go for a walk."

"Boo!"

I ignore the boos and throw a few bills down on the table before leading Indigo outside. She shivers when the wind hits us and I use the excuse to wrap an arm around her shoulders. I consider it a victory when she doesn't brush me off.

"Time's up," she says when we reach the end of Main Street and turn left.

I'm not ready to discuss my family, but if there's one person who will understand it's Indigo. "I found my dad."

She gasps. "You did? How? Your mom never gave you a clue who he was."

"I did one of those DNA tests. When a possible match came up, I hired a lawyer to do some research."

Her smile stretches from ear to ear. "I'm happy for you. You always wanted to find your family."

I clear my throat. "There's more."

"Okay."

"My dad was married when he was with my mom." Her eyes widen but she doesn't speak. "And he had five other children. Actually six," I correct when I remember what the little girl said.

"You have six brothers?"

"Half-brothers," I correct.

"Whatever. This is amazing. A family! It's what you've always wanted."

What I wanted was to make a family with her. But I screwed up and walked away from her.

"Hold on. You said had." She bites her lip. "Is your dad gone?"

"He died a few years before I found him."

She clutches my hands. "I'm sorry."

I clear my throat. "They're here."

"Here?" Her brow wrinkles. "Your brothers are here? As in Winter Falls?"

"Yeah."

She bounces on her toes. "Have you met them? What are they like?"

"I haven't met them yet." I pause. I don't want to admit my fears, but if there's anyone who won't judge me it's this woman. "What if they don't like me?"

She squeezes my hands. "They'd be stupid not to like you. You're awesome."

My chest warms at her words. "Maybe, but I'm not ready."

"There's no rush. You've waited this long. You can wait a little longer. If you need time to come to grips with the situation, take it."

This is why I love this woman. She understands me. She supports me. She doesn't push me. She stands by my side and gives me what I need.

With a start I realize I not merely love this woman – have always loved this woman – but I'm still in love with her. I probably always will be.

Did I screw up when I left her? Should I have stayed with her no matter what? Knowing she deserves better than me?

Chapter 10

Invasion – When the brothers you've never met get tired of waiting for you and crash into your life

Cash

"I'll get it," Indigo shouts when the doorbell rings the next day.

I don't try to stop her as she barrels down the stairs. The doorbell has rung nearly constantly since she arrived. The gossip gals were the first but they weren't the last. Indigo wasn't exaggerating when she said the refrigerator is bursting with food.

"Who are you?"

"We're here to see Cash."

Shit. Are my half-brothers here? Moon wasn't kidding when she said my time's up.

I tiptoe to the edge of the hallway and peek around the corner. Indigo is standing with her hands on her hips facing down five men. All of whom faintly resemble me.

"You didn't answer my question."

"Darling, can you please get Cash for us?"

"Why?"

"We know he's home."

"Trust us. He wants to see us."

"No, he doesn't."

My heart warms at her words. She's staring down five men all of whom are practically a foot taller than her and she's doing it for me. Because I told her I wasn't ready to meet my family.

I was an idiot to ever let this woman go. Not anymore. I'm done being an idiot. Indy will be mine again. As soon as I can convince her to forgive me for breaking her heart.

Lucky for me we're stuck living together in this house. Plenty of time for me to remind her why she fell in love with me.

Indy pushes the door to shut it, but one of the men sticks out his foot to stop her. "Can you tell Cash we're here to see him?"

She growls at him. "Move your foot before I call the police."

"I like her!"

"She's got spunk!"

"She needs it with this family."

I hurry down the hallway. As much fun as it is to watch Indy defend me, I should be the one protecting her. Not the other way around.

I place my hand on her lower back. "It's okay."

She studies me. "Are you sure? Yesterday you said you weren't ready to meet them."

"I'm sure. Thanks for holding them off but I've got this." I kiss her nose.

"I thought the gossip gals said they weren't a couple," one of them mumbles.

Indy glares at him. "Do you know what we do with little boys who talk when they shouldn't?"

He taps his cheek. "Give them kisses?"

"Don't make me put you on the naughty seat in the corner."

He waggles his eyebrows. "Will you be joining me?"

"Enough!" I wrap an arm around Indy before shoving her behind me. "Did you come here to flirt with my wo— Indy?"

His response? He smiles. Is he crazy?

"I'll let you handle them," Indy whispers before leaving me alone with my half-brothers. I wait until a door upstairs closes before facing them.

"What are you doing here?"

"I'm guessing since you didn't want to see us that you know who we are?" The man who I saw with the little blonde girl asks.

I cross my arms over my chest. "I know who you are."

"Shall I make the introductions out here where the gossip gals can watch? Or shall we go inside?"

I scan the area and sure enough, Petal is standing on the porch across the street with binoculars. I scowl before motioning the men inside. "Come in."

We gather in the living room.

"I should probably introduce these yahoos. I'm Damon." He motions to the identical twins lounging on the sofa. "Riley and Brody. They're the youngest."

"I'm older than Brody," Riley says.

Brody pinches him. "By two minutes, dipshit."

"Older is older."

Damon clears his throat. "The big guy standing in the corner is Miller."

"You can call him the King Grump," Brody says and Miller growls at him.

"And this is Elder." Damon points to the last man standing. "Miller and Elder are fraternal twins."

We're missing one brother. "Where's Peace?"

Brody rolls his eyes. "Mr. Stuck In The Mud didn't approve of our mission."

Mission? Meeting me is a mission? They don't want to meet me? To get to know me?

Riley elbows him. "Peace is on duty."

"Told ya. Stuck in the mud."

"How do you know about Peace?" Damon asks.

"Your little girl told me."

The pride is clear to see in his smile.

"We should have some kind of induction ceremony," Elder says.

"Induction ceremony?" I ask.

"Yeah. To introduce new brothers into the Bragg Brother Bunch."

I swallow. "There are more of us?"

He shrugs. "There are bound to be."

"No." Damon shakes his head. "Cash is the last Bragg brother."

"How do you know?" I ask.

Before he can answer, the devil cat saunters into the room. She hisses at me before jumping onto the sofa between Riley and Brody.

"What does the cat say after making a joke?" Elder asks. His brothers' groans don't stop him. "Just kitten!"

"Don't worry," Riley says as he picks up the cat and cuddles her close. "His jokes are harmless."

I gape at him. "You're cuddling the devil cat."

He scratches behind her ears. "She's not the devil."

Brody reaches to pet her and she swipes at him. "Devil cat."

Miller growls. "Can you stop discussing the cat and allow Damon to explain why he knows there are no more Bragg brothers out there?"

Brody raises his hand. "I, for one, would be happy to discover there are no more Bragg brothers."

My stomach falls. They don't want me. I finally found my family and they don't want me. Fucking hell. Why did I go in search of my father? The band is my family. I don't need anyone else.

Riley glares at Brody. "Don't be an asshole. Now Cash thinks we're rejecting him."

"I don't think you're rejecting me," I lie.

Brody frowns. "Sorry. I didn't mean to imply I didn't want to meet you. I just wish Dad would have learned to keep it in his pants."

I can't help myself. I sit on the chair next to the sofa and lean toward him. I've always wanted to know about my dad. "Keep it in his pants?"

"Dad never heard of the word faithful."

I know this since he had an affair with my mom when he was married to their mom. But he didn't go around sleeping with women all the time, did he?

"My mom loved him," I murmur. She put him on a pedestal and when he fell off it, she dove into a bottle and never came up for air again.

"Ah crap. I'm sorry. I didn't mean… It's …" He blows out a puff of air.

"What Brody is trying to say is our dad had a habit of having affairs with women," Damon says. "But I'm sure he cared for your mom."

Silence falls and I scan the faces of my half-brothers. None of them will meet my gaze. They know their brother's lying to try and make me feel better.

"It's okay. You don't have to soften the blow. I figured my dad was an asshole after my mom died when I was a minor and he sicced his lawyers on social services when they tried to get him to accept custody of me."

My lawyer dug up that little gem. While I was roaming the streets, trying to find places to sleep after Mom died, I had a Dad who refused to accept me. Who didn't bother to meet me when I had no one else.

"Dad was an asshole," Miller growls.

"What happened to you?" Damon asks. "Did you go into care?"

I shrug like the whole situation wasn't a big deal. Like I wasn't terrified where my next meal was coming from. "I was seventeen and a senior in high school. I stayed with friends until I graduated."

"And then you formed *Cash & the Sinners* and became a huge success." Riley grins. "Our brother is a freaking rockstar."

I squirm in my seat. I don't want to be Cash, the rockstar, to these men. I want to be their brother. Part of their family. I want to experience the easy rapport I have with my band with them.

"Hey," Indy enters the room. "Everything going okay in here?" She glares at each of my brothers in turn.

I stand and tag her hand. "Everything's fine. These are my brothers. Damon, Brody, Riley, Elder, and Miller."

She smiles at them. "Nice to meet you." She lowers her voice. "Are you okay? Did you need me to kick them out of the house?"

I squeeze her hand. "I'm fine."

She studies my face for a moment before nodding. "Okay. I've got errands to do. I'll be back in a while."

"Bye, boys." She waves.

"Hot damn. She's gorgeous."

I whirl around to growl at Riley. He holds up his hands. "Don't worry. I'm happy in my relationship."

"We all are," Brody adds.

I sit on my chair and they tell me all about their love stories. As I listen, I can't help but think of Indy. I don't want our love story to be over. I want a second chance. And I'm getting it. I'm not letting her slip through my fingers again.

She's mine. She always has been.

Chapter 11

Jerk face – Someone who lets information about an intimate moment slip to band mates who aren't known for their discretion

INDIGO

"Go away," a man shouts after I knock on the door.

My response? I knock again.

"Go away!"

"I'm here to see Dylan," I announce through the door.

"He doesn't want to see you!"

Because he doesn't know who it is. I start knocking and don't stop until the door opens.

I wish I could say I don't know who this person is. Could claim I've been able to ignore any mention of Cash's band for the past decade. But I can't. It's hard to ignore a picture of your ex on the front cover of a magazine when you're at the grocery check-out lane. Switching lanes doesn't work. Trust me. I've tried.

This is Jett – drummer for the world famous *Cash & the Sinners* band. He glares at me for all of a microsecond before he bites his lip and rakes his gaze over me. Freaking rockstars.

"Look, darling, Dylan's not interested, but you can give me your number."

I roll my eyes. "I'm here to see Dylan," I repeat.

"Dylan doesn't fuck fans." He wiggles his eyebrows. "But I do."

"Not interested. Tell Dylan Indigo's here."

All signs of Jett the flirt disappear. "Indigo?"

"Dylan!" I shout since Jett's being a major unhelpful pain in the butt.

"Indigo? Is that you?" Dylan pushes Jett out of his way. "It is you!"

He picks me up and twirls me around while chanting, "Indigo! Indigo! Indigo!"

I giggle when he sets me down. "Dylan. Dylan. Dylan."

"This is Indigo? *The* Indigo?" Jet asks.

Dylan wraps an arm around my shoulders and hauls me near. "Indigo, this is Jet. I'd say watch out for him since he'll hit on you, but he already did."

Jet holds up his palms and retreats a few steps. "It was a joke. I didn't know who she was."

I lean close to mock-whisper to Dylan, "What's his problem?"

"He thinks Cash will beat his ass for hitting on you."

"Cash doesn't care who hits on me."

"Have you forgotten how he beat up the soccer player for winking at you?"

"Cash didn't beat him up." Dylan raises an eyebrow. "He didn't," I insist, although Cash totally did beat up the poor soccer player.

"How did you know I'm in Winter Falls? Does Cash know you're here? What are you doing here anyway?"

I ignore the first two questions – I came here to escape Cash, not discuss him – and answer the last one, "My grandma lived here."

"Lived?"

My eyes itch but I sniff to hold back the tears. "She passed away a week ago." Will those words ever get any easier to say?

He wraps me up in a hug. "I'm sorry, Indigo."

The door flies open. "Indigo's here?"

"She does exist!"

Dylan releases me and spins me around to face the new arrivals. "This is Fender and Gibson."

Fender lifts his chin in greeting while Gibson saunters my way. He holds out his hand, but he doesn't shake mine. He presses his lips to my fingers instead.

"Charmed to make your acquaintance."

Fender smacks him upside the head. "No hitting on Cash's girl."

"I'm not Cash's girl." No matter how much my stomach warms upon hearing the words. Or how much I enjoyed kissing him the other day. Or how much I want to touch those muscles he's developed since high school.

I'm not giving Cash the chance to break my heart again. And he would break it again since nothing's changed. He still values his rockstar life over me.

Fender snorts. "You'll always be Cash's girl."

I haven't been Cash's girl since he walked away at our high school graduation ceremony. But I'm not discussing my relationship with Cash with a bunch of rockstars I barely know. Time for a diversion.

"Is Fender your real name?" I wave toward Gibson. "What about you? Gibson your real name?"

Gibson ignores my question – he probably assumes I already know everything about the band – and grasps my hand to lead me to the sofa where he pushes me down and sits right next to me.

For the record, I don't know everything about *Cash & the Sinners*. I didn't cyberstalk them like some overenthusiastic fan girl. In fact, I may have switched the radio station a time or two or three thousand when one of their songs came on the air.

"Tell us everything," Gibson insists. "What was Cash like as a teenager?"

"Why are you asking me? Dylan went to high school with Cash."

He sticks out his bottom lip and pouts. "But he refuses to give us any blackmail material."

Dylan grunts. "Don't expect Indigo to give you any either."

"Many more qualified journalists than you have tried," I taunt.

Dylan frowns. "Sorry about them."

I shrug. "You're not responsible for the actions of others."

"Cash lost it when he found out about the reporter who snuck into your house and was laying on your bed in wait."

Cash knows what happened? Why didn't he phone or contact me? Why didn't he—

Nope. Shutting those thoughts down. It wasn't Cash's responsibility to contact me even if it was his fault I was being harassed.

"What happened?" Jett asks.

"Some jerk thought it was okay to climb into my window to harass me."

"Fucking paps," Fender grumbles.

"He didn't hurt you, did he?" Jett asks.

"Nope." I smirk. "And he learned his lesson when Katy Purry decided his fingers were cat treats."

"Katy Purry?"

"My cat."

Jett mock shivers. "You named your cat after a pop singer?"

I wag my finger at him. "Don't you start. It's bad enough Cash thinks Katy Purry is the devil."

Dylan leans closer to me. "Cash has met your cat?"

Shoot. I clamp my mouth shut. I wasn't planning on telling Mr. Nosy about my current living situation.

"It all makes sense now," Dylan mutters.

Jett glances back and forth between Dylan and me. "What makes sense?"

"Why we're in Winter Falls. It didn't have anything to do with Cash's family. It was all about Indigo."

I wag my finger at Dylan. "Nuh-uh. Don't you go blaming me. I didn't know you would be here."

"Hold on. You said family. Cash doesn't have any family." Gibson stares at me. "Does he?"

I hold up my hand. "What are you asking me for? I'm not some romance heroine who got pregnant with Cash's baby, never told him, and now there's a mini-Cash in the world he doesn't know about."

He frowns. "If you aren't the family Dylan means, who else could it be?"

I glare at Dylan. He had to open his big fat mouth. He must know Cash found his biological father. He avoids my gaze and stalks toward the kitchen. "Who wants a beer?"

"Let's order a pizza," Jett suggests.

"How long have you been in Winter Falls?" I ask.

"Long enough to know there's no pizza delivery," Gibson answers.

"We can go to *Naked Falls Brewing*."

The door opens and Cash strolls inside. I check him over. No signs of bloodshed. Good. He didn't get into a fight with his brothers.

He smiles when he notices me. "Hey, Indy. What are you doing here?"

"Came to catch up with your better half."

Dylan hands me a beer. "It's true. I am the better half. I'm also prettier than him."

Gibson puffs out his chest. "Everyone knows I'm the pretty one in the band."

"I believe the fans disagree. At last count, I was winning," Jett declares.

"Winning? Winning what?" I ask.

Jett's eyes widen and he stutters. "U-u-um…nothing."

"Nothing? I guess you aren't winning after all." Gibson smirks at him.

"Do I want to know what you're talking about?"

Cash chuckles. "No, you don't." He perches himself on the arm of the sofa and squeezes my shoulder. "Thanks for what you did."

"What did she do?" Dylan asks.

Jett waggles his eyebrows. "Did she let you pet her kitty?"

My cheeks warm as I remember how Cash kissed me a few days ago. How I would have let him drag me to the nearest horizontal surface if Katy Purry hadn't interrupted us.

Jett motions toward my face. "He did pet her kitty."

Cash punches his shoulder. "Don't talk about Indy's kitty."

Jett bats his eyelashes. Does he think anyone's buying his innocent act? I'm not. "I was referring to Katy Purry."

"She's the devil," Cash mutters.

"My cat is not the devil."

"Didn't your cat eat the pap's fingers?" Gibson asks.

"She didn't eat them, eat them. Maybe nibbled on them a bit."

Cash's forehead wrinkles. "Why would the demon cat attack a pap?" I don't get a chance to answer before he growls. "Is this the pap who invaded your home?"

"Don't growl at me." I shove him off the arm of the sofa. "You're not allowed to get annoyed with me because a pap came after me for information about you."

He crosses his arms over his chest and glares down at me. "Why the hell not?"

I jump to my feet. "Because you left me. My life doesn't have anything to do with yours."

"It sure the hell does. You're mine."

"I am not yours." He reaches for me but I bat him away. "Don't touch me. I didn't give you permission to touch me."

"You didn't seem to mind the other day."

I can't believe him. Did he seriously announce to his bandmates how we had a moment a few days ago?

"Don't be a jerk face," I growl at him before waving to Dylan. "We'll catch up another time."

"I'll be here."

"Don't go," Jett pouts. "I'm enjoying the show."

I ignore him and march out of the apartment. I hear Cash chasing after me and quicken my pace.

"Indigo!"

At his shout, I start running. I can't believe I nearly fell into his trap again. What was I thinking?

Chapter 12

Goat – May be used as a cock blocker if you're losing a bet

CASH

I chase after Indy as she rushes down the hallway and out the front door of the apartment building. She glances back at me and notices I'm catching up before increasing her pace.

I should probably let her go. But I need to apologize. I should have never said anything about our kiss to the guys. I'm an idiot. But when she said she isn't mine, I lost it. I wanted to remind her of what we had. Of what we can have again. Because I'm not letting her go. Not this time.

"Indy!"

I shout after her and she increases her pace. I don't know what she's thinking. There's no way she can outrun me. My long legs eat up the distance between us in no time.

"Indy." I reach for her and she bats me away. I lift my hands in surrender. "Can we please talk?"

She stops and places her hands on her knees as she struggles for breath. "Talk. About. What?"

"The reason you fled Dylan's apartment."

"I didn't flee," she claims between gasps for breath.

I cock an eyebrow.

She scowls at me. "I didn't flee."

"You were running down the street for fun?"

She stands up straight. "Yep. You got it in one. I now run for fun."

"You run for fun? The same girl who tried to give herself food poisoning to get out of gym class?"

"I didn't try to give myself food poisoning."

"You drank the spoiled milk for fun?"

"Maybe I didn't realize the milk had gone bad."

"The big chunks didn't give it away?"

She fists her hands on her hips. "Why are we discussing the ancient past?"

I open my mouth to say she started it but snap it closed again when I realize how childish arguing about who started what sounds.

"Can we talk?"

"We don't have anything to discuss."

Those words sting but I ignore the pain. Indy's lashing out at me because I hurt her. This is my fault and I need to accept responsibility.

"I'm sorry I mentioned we kissed to my band."

She crosses her arms over her chest. The movement pushes her breasts up and I nearly groan at the sight. I love all of Indy's curves but her breasts are my favorite.

"How dare you tell your band about us kissing? It was private. You may live your life in the limelight, but I don't. And I don't want to."

Her words give me pause. Should I stop my pursuit of her? She doesn't want to live her life in the public's eye and I don't have a choice but to live my life in the public's eye.

But when I gaze into her hazel eyes blazing with anger, I know I won't give her up. Not again. I went down that road once and it led me straight to hell.

"I'm sorry. I was wrong. It won't happen again."

"Darn right, it won't because you and I won't be kissing again."

We sure the hell will be kissing again – we'll be doing a lot more than kissing – but I don't say those words out loud. Despite the stupid things I've said over the past hour, I'm not a complete idiot.

"And I am not yours."

Indy is mine, but I jumped the gun by announcing it in front of her and the band. I need to have patience – a trait I am not known for. I need time to convince Indy to give me another chance. But I will convince her.

I shrug my shoulders and feign nonchalance. "You were mine."

"But I'm not anymore. I haven't been yours for a long time."

"I never should have let you go," I murmur.

"Why did you let me go?"

Shit. I'm not admitting why I left her. I'm never admitting the truth. It would break her heart. And I'm done hurting her.

"I was an idiot."

She rolls her eyes. "Duh."

Relief fills me. She's letting it go.

"You being an idiot is given, but what reason did your idiot brain come up with for dumping me?"

Damn. She's not letting it go.

"Can't you just let it go?"

Her eyes narrow and I realize I'm being an idiot again. Indigo Scott doesn't let anything go.

"I don't know why I try with you. If you can't be honest with me, we can't be friends."

I smile. "We're friends?"

"Do you have a hearing problem? I literally said we can't be friends five seconds ago."

"All I heard was friends."

"Must be nice having selective hearing. You can go about your merry way without worrying about anyone or anything. You don't have to concern yourself with paparazzi showing up at your house, invading your private sanctuary."

I growl. "I'm sorry that idiot broke into your house."

She snorts. "Yeah, sorry. Sure, you are."

"I am sorry."

"Which is why you rang to check on me? And made sure I had a security system to prevent someone from breaking into my apartment ever again?"

"I—"

She holds up her hand. "Never mind. It's stupid. Why would the great Cash Evans – international rockstar who can do no wrong even when he's fleeing naked from the cops – check on little 'ole me – boring elementary school teacher with too many curves to count?"

I tuck a strand of her silky smooth hair behind her ear. "First of all, I *allegedly* fled naked from the cops." Her lips tip up in an almost smile. "Secondly, I can count your curves. I'd spend days and days counting your curves if you'd let me."

Her eyes flare with heat before she clears her throat and retreats. "And yet you didn't check on me when I was attacked in my own home."

"I did check on you," I growl.

"Was I awake at the time?" she sasses.

"Smart ass. I knew you wouldn't accept my phone calls. I contacted your landlord instead. Who do you think paid to have a new security system installed in your apartment?"

Her mouth drops open. "Y-y-ou?"

I use a finger on her jaw to close her mouth. "I'm not a complete asshole. It was my fault the scumbag was after you."

"You should have told me."

"Would you have spoken to me?"

"Maybe."

"Liar." Indigo Scott is not only strong and sassy. She's stubborn as hell.

She inhales a deep breath. "Thank you for ensuring my safety."

This woman slays me. She's hurt I didn't personally contact her when the scumbag reporter broke into her house and yet here she is thanking me for getting her a new security system.

Damn. I love her. I've always loved her. I was a fool to let her go. A young fool who let another person make a decision for him. I won't make the same mistake again.

"You're welcome." I crowd her. "Whatever you need, Indy, I will always make sure you have it. Always."

Her hazel eyes warm as she gazes up at me. My gaze dips to her bowtie lips. Her breath hitches and I dip my head.

Baaa!

I startle at the sound of a goat's bleating.

"Is there a couple walking a goat on a leash or did Dylan put some kind of hallucinogen in my beer?" she asks.

The couple waves at us from across the street. "Nope. It's real."

"Okay then." She blinks and the heat and warmth in her eyes disappear. "Thanks for explaining about the security system. I need to…" She motions toward the street. "I need to … I'll see you."

I watch as she scurries away. Damn. I missed my chance.

I stuff my hands in my pockets and head toward her grandmother's house. Never mind. We're living in the same house. I'll get another chance.

I whistle as I stroll down the sidewalk.

Chapter 13

Bragg Brother Group Text

Brody: Welcome to the Bragg Brother Bunch.

Cash: Who is this? How did you get my number?

Riley: Brody can get anyone's number. It's his super power.

Brody: I have other super powers. Ask Soleil. She knows.

Damon: Can we get to the point of this conversation?

Cash: What is going on?

Brody: We're welcoming you to our brotherhood.

Peace: Don't bother trying to fight it. It won't do you any good.

Miller: They'll just follow you around until you give in.

Elder: I think you mean 'we'.

Miller: Nope.

Elder: You'll get used to my twin. He's a grumpy asshole but we love him.

Damon: Because we have to.

Cash: Is there a reason for this group text?

Brody: Does there need to be a reason to reach out to your brothers?

Riley: Nope. We're family.

Elder: I shook my family tree and a bunch of nuts fell out.

Cash: Are his jokes supposed to be funny?

Elder: I amuse myself.

Miller: And no one else.

Elder: Robin thinks I'm funny.

Miller: Robin is a baby.

Elder: Harmony thinks I'm funny.

Damon: Harmony pretends you're funny. It's what wives do.

Elder: How do you know? Are you secretly married and didn't tell us?

Damon: Are you ever going to let how I kept Skye a secret go?

Brody: No!

Riley: No!

Elder: No!

Miller: No.

Peace: You never should have kept Skye's existence a secret.

Damon: Like you didn't try to keep Olivia's pregnancy a secret.

Peace: Not the same thing.

Riley: Especially since you can't keep a secret in Winter Falls anyway.

Cash: Keeping secrets is bad news.

Brody: Oh really?

Elder: If keeping secrets is bad news, you can tell us all about why you had a knock-down, drag-out fight with your woman on the sidewalk yesterday.

Cash: What are you talking about?

Brody: Isn't he cute? Thinking we don't already know.

Peace: Warning. Brody probably dug into your private life.

Cash: Not possible.

Brody: I disagree. Also, on a totally unrelated note, you should speak to Damon about investing your money. Keeping cash in the bank is a waste of capital.

Cash: Who the hell do you think you are?

Brody: I'm your brother. You're older brother.

Riley: He's been waiting thirty years to be an older brother.

Cash: Brother or not, it's not okay to dig into my financial records.

Peace: Can you please not discuss Brody breaking the law around me?

Brody: Who says I broke the law?

Peace: Don't bullshit me, Brody Bragg. I know you.

Brody: And I know I have a list of every single girlfriend you've had since you were ten I'm dying to give to Olivia.

Peace: You wouldn't.

Cash: What's the big deal? Surely, your girlfriend knows you had other girlfriends before her.

Riley: Olivia's a nut. She'd probably form a Girlfriends of Peace support group.

Brody: They'd meet up and discuss all things Peace.

Peace: If I promise to let this offense slide, will you promise to burn the list, Brody?

Brody: I think you mean indiscretion not offense.

Peace: Whatever.

Damon: I thought today's discussion was supposed to be about Cash and Indigo.

Cash: My relationship with Indy is none of your business.

Riley: He's cute.

Elder: Absolutely adorable.

Brody: He'll learn quick enough. There are no secrets in Winter Falls.

Cash: Good thing I don't live in Winter Falls.

Damon: But how are you going to get the girl if you don't live in Winter Falls?

Peace: I hate to agree with them, but they're right. Indigo lives in Winter Falls. You need to be here if you want a relationship with her.

Miller: You do want a relationship with her, don't you? You're not using her, are you?

Cash: No! I'm not using Indy. I would never use Indy.

Brody: But you dumped her on graduation day.

Cash: How the hell do you know that?

Riley: My twin can find out anything.

Brody: Twin powers....

Riley: ...activate!

Damon: You left her on graduation day??? I thought rockstars were supposed to be smooth operators.

Cash: I wasn't a rockstar back in high school.

Damon: Ah, I get it.

Cash: Get what?

Damon: You left her to seek fame and fortune.

Elder: Why are rockstars so cool? Because they have tons of fans.

Miller: Please ignore my twin.

Cash: I did not leave Indy to become a rockstar.

Riley: Then, why did you dump her?

Cash: None of your business.

Miller: Tell us or this group text will never end.

Cash: I'm serious. It's none of your business.

Brody: Don't make me find out.

Peace: Please don't make Brody find out.

Cash: You won't figure it out no matter how much you breach my privacy.

Damon: You had to poke the dragon.

Brody: I'm the dragon!

Damon: It's a metaphor.

Brody: Nope! No take backs. I'm a dragon. The end.

Cash: I need to get back to work.

Brody: Oh please. Now you're insulting me. I know you're not at the recording studio today.

Cash: Maybe I need to write some songs for the new album. Ever think of that?

Riley: You cured your writer's block?

Elder: I bet Indigo cured his writer's block.

Cash: How the hell do you know about my writer's block?

Brody: Welcome to Winter Falls.

Cash: Not sure I want to stay here if everyone's going to be in my business all the time.

Damon: You're staying?

Cash: I have an album to record.

Riley: I guess you better write some songs.

Brody: We'll leave it to you, bro.

Peace: Are the wonder twins actually being reasonable?

Damon: No. They're up to something.

Cash has left the conversation.

Brody: He's cute. I'll let him think he can leave the conversation. For now.

Chapter 14

Writer's block – An inability to write a love song because you're too busy trying to live a long song

INDIGO

"What are you doing?"

I startle at Cash's question and nearly drop the box I'm carrying.

"What does it look like I'm doing?" I nod toward the boxes on the floor.

"You're cleaning out your grandmother's house?"

"Ding. Ding. Ding. Got it one go!"

"But why? If you're going to live here for a year, won't you need things?"

I roll my eyes. "I hardly need five hundred Harlequin romance books."

"You don't? I remember you used to inhale your mom's old romance books."

Of course, he remembers. Those books would make me all hot and bothered; itching with sexual need. And Cash was always ready and willing to help me work away the need. After he fanned the flames first. My face warms as the memories assault me.

I clear my throat. "Not anymore."

Cash smirks when he notices how red my face is. Lucky for him and his man parts, he doesn't remark upon it. "You didn't deny you're going to live here for a year."

I open my mouth to deny it now, but what's the use? He figured out I was staying in Winter Falls long before I was ready to admit it to myself. Naturally, I'm staying. I can't let Grandma's house be demolished. Even if I have to put my life on hold for a year. What's a year to save the house Grandma loved?

I sigh. "Because I'm staying."

He grins. "I knew you would."

"Don't be a braggart. No one likes a showoff."

He winks. "But I'm really good at showing off."

I snort. "I bet you are."

I carry the box to the hallway to join the pile of boxes I already placed there. When I return to the living room, Cash is emptying a shelf.

"What are you doing?"

"I'm helping."

I don't want his help. Every time I'm around Cash, the wall I've built around my heart – the one with the big flashing 'Cash Stay Out' sign – cracks. I need him to stay away before it crumbles completely. This isn't some second chance romance in the making.

"Aren't you supposed to be recording an album or doing some other rockstar stuff?"

He chuckles. "Rockstar stuff?"

"You know – smashing guitars, sleeping with your fans, getting drunk as a skunk."

"I don't get drunk."

Shootawhoota. I'm a jerk. I know he doesn't get drunk.

"I'm sorry."

"Nothing to be sorry about. At least you won't try to force me to drink tequila shots off your belly button."

My nose wrinkles. "Who would ask you to…" I stop myself when I realize there are thousands of fans who would ask him to drink shots off their bodies. Probably their naked bodies. I do not need to know about any of it. "Never mind."

"It's nice, you know."

"What's nice? Having millions of fans?"

I grit my teeth. What is he getting at? First, he left me to become a rockstar and now he's bragging about his fans. Geez. Way to make a girl feel special.

"Nice being around someone who understands why I don't touch tequila or vodka or any of the other hard stuff."

I amend my earlier statement. Cash does know how to make a girl feel special. I want to gather him into my arms and hold him close. Erase all his pain from having an alcoholic for a mom. A woman who chose the bottle over her son when she drank herself into an early grave.

But I won't. Cash isn't mine to hold and comfort. He's my past. Not my present. Not my future. I need to keep distance between the two of us. I have no idea how I'm going to manage it since we'll be living in this house together for the foreseeable future. How long does it take to record an album anyway?

"How long are you planning to stay in Winter Falls?"

He glances over his shoulder at me. "Trying to get rid of me already?"

"I've been trying to get rid of you since I arrived or have you forgotten?"

He feigns a shiver. "Forgotten how you're using the demon cat to run me out of house and home? Not likely."

"Katy Purry is a sweetheart. You should give her a chance."

"A chance to eat my fingers like sausages? No thanks."

I roll my eyes. "Don't exaggerate."

"She left you another present this morning. A baby bird with its head cut off."

I gasp. "Not a baby bird." I refuse to believe it. He's winding me up. "It was probably already dead. Baby birds fall out of their nests all the time. It's sad but it happens."

"You believe whatever you need to believe. But don't say I didn't warn you when Satan shows up for your soul."

"Now, I've sold my soul to Satan via my cat? Katy Purry would never steal my soul."

"Sure, she wouldn't." He stands with the box in his hand. "Where do you want this?"

"In the hallway."

I fill the next box while he carries the full one away. "Grandma. Grandma. Grandma," I tsk at the amount of books she had with Fabio on the front cover.

Grandma always did have a thing for men with long hair. She even tried to get Grandpa to grow his hair long. He refused and then when he went bald, she bought him a wig for 'play time'. I stopped paying attention to her love of long-haired men after those words were uttered.

Grandma and Grandpa did not have sex. Mom was born via immaculate conception or was adopted or brought by the stork. Anything but the result of s-e-x between my sweet elderly grandparents.

"Where are you taking all of these books?" Cash asks as he pulls books off the shelves.

"They're going to the library. I contacted *Fall Into A Good Book,* the bookstore Grandma used to own, but the new owner didn't want them. She only sells new books and doesn't have the shelf room for these old paperbacks."

"I didn't know your grandma used to own a bookstore."

"Grandma loved the bookstore but after she broke her hip a few years ago, she couldn't keep up with it and sold it."

I can't believe I didn't come visit Grandma when she broke her hip. I chose a stupid summer course in my master's program over my grandma. If only I had known how little time she had left. How little time we had left together.

"Did your mom come to Winter Falls to help your grandma?"

I sigh. "Mom and Grandma haven't spoken for years. Don't ask me what they fought over. I don't know. Neither one of them would tell me."

Silence falls as we finish emptying the bookshelf.

"That's the last one," I say as I close the final box.

I stand but my legs are half-asleep from sitting for such a long time and I sway as my knees buckle. Cash catches me before I can crumble to the floor.

"Careful, Indy. You don't want to fall and knock yourself out and give Devil Cat the opportunity to eat your face."

I shove him away. "Be nice or I'll train Katy Purry to pee all over your favorite Chucks."

He gasps and clutches his chest. "You wouldn't."

I mock glare at him. "Try me."

He sighs. "I guess I better behave."

"You? Behave? That'll be the day."

"Hey! I can behave. I prefer not to. But I can do it."

"Whatever." I check the time on my watch. "It's too late to deliver the boxes to the library today. It'll be closed by now. I guess I'll do it tomorrow."

"I'll help."

"You don't need to. I'm fine to do it by myself."

He crosses his arms over his chest and I keep my eyes glued to his face. I will not ogle his chest or his arms. Ogling is bad.

"I'm not letting you carry all these boxes on your own."

Forget about those muscles. They belong to a jerk face!

"Let me? You're not my owner. I'm not your chattel. You don't *let me* do anything. I do what I want."

He rubs a hand down his face. "Bad choice of words."

I raise my eyebrows and cross my arms over my chest. "Really?"

"I meant to ask if you'd allow me to help."

As much as I'd appreciate his help – my arms are the consistency of noodles after carrying the boxes a mere few feet – I need to keep my distance from this man. And he needs to stop being nice! I can't resist Mr. Nice Guy Cash.

"Aren't you supposed to be recording an album?"

He glances away but not before I notice the pink coloring his cheeks. What's he got to be embarrassed about?

Don't tell me he lied to me about the album. "You are recording an album, aren't you?"

He clears his throat. "Yep. I need to work on some lyrics is all."

"You mean you don't have a gazillion songs already written in the tatty notebook you always carry around?"

He used to scribble lyrics in his notebook at the most random of times. We'd finish a round of love making and he'd kiss me before grabbing his notebook. I never could figure out if I should be flattered or offended.

"Hey, I don't use a tatty notebook anymore."

He's also avoiding the subject. "What's wrong? Writer's block got you down?"

He scowls and I gasp.

"You're kidding. You never had writer's block before."

He shrugs. "There's a first time for everything."

"I'm sorry. It must be shitty to be blocked from doing what you love the most in the world."

"Writing music isn't what I love most in the world," he murmurs.

I don't ask because I don't want to find out that singing to crowds in a stadium is what he loves most. How could I ever compete with thousands of adoring fans?

Ugh! Knock it off, Indigo. I don't want to compete, remember? There's a wall around my heart with Do Not Enter signs posted on it for a reason.

"You want to watch a movie?"

"As long as it's not some costume drama."

I giggle. We're totally watching a costume drama.

Chapter 15

Front door – For use by gossip gals and neighbors, not bandmates

CASH

The movie begins to play and the first scene is of some dude in a chariot wearing a corset. Men should not wear corsets.

I groan. "What the hell is this?"

Indy widens her eyes. "Whatever do you mean?"

"Innocent? You're going to play innocent with me?"

She bats her eyelashes. "What?"

"You've done it now." I launch myself at her and tickle her ribs.

She squirms and bats at me. "Stop it!"

"Admit you chose a costume drama to torture me."

"No! Never!"

She falls back and I climb on top of her. I pause when I realize I've got her right where I want her. My body blankets hers and her breasts rub against my chest as she fights for breath. Heaven. This is heaven.

I forget all about tickling her as my gaze zooms in on her lips. Her perfect lips with their bowtie shape. She bites her bottom lip and I groan.

"I'm going to kiss you now," I announce but I don't give her a chance to reply before my lips meet hers.

I start with a soft touch. I don't want to press her too hard too fast. She'll run away if I do.

But when she sighs and her mouth opens, soft goes out the window. I push my tongue into her mouth and cock my head to the side before I dive in. Her strawberry and cream taste hits me and I moan. She always tastes of candy with a side of wicked. It's addicting.

I cradle her face in my hands as I reacquaint myself with every inch of her mouth. Her tongue duels with mine and I groan before turning the heat up on the kiss.

Her legs fall open and I press my hard length into her center. She moves to wrap her legs around me and something crashes to the ground before the television blares.

"A society on the brink of change finds its fate entwined in the dance of romance and scandal."

I reach for the remote to switch off the sound, but I'm too late. Indy is already pushing on my shoulders in a silent demand for me to get off her. I sit up with a sigh.

She jumps to her feet and marches toward the staircase. "So much for the Cash stay out signs," she grumbles as she flees.

I watch as she rushes up the stairs, but I don't follow. I've pressed her enough for the day. Bit by bit I'm tearing down those walls she's erected against me.

I groan and collapse against the sofa. It's going to be another cold shower for me tonight.

I hum as I return to my bedroom after my shower. My fingers itch for my guitar as the start of a chorus flits through my mind. It's there but slightly beyond my reach.

I settle on a chair with my guitar on my lap and strum a few chords.

I've always known

You're the one I need

Not quite it. I clear my throat and change the key.

I've learned from my mistakes

I've grown

I've always known

Getting there. I continue to work on the song until I'm satisfied with the lyrics. I'll play it for the guys tomorrow and we'll refine the music. Jett can add some drums, Fender some bass, and Gibson some rhythm. It's how we usually make my lyrics into a song since writing music is not my strength.

Something hits the window and I glance over expecting to see the devil cat staring at me with her beady eyes. But it's Dylan waving at me with a goofy grin on his face.

"What are you doing here?" I ask when I open the window.

"Thought I'd stop by."

"We're not teenagers anymore. You can use the front door."

"I didn't want to wake Indigo."

"Liar."

"Fine," he huffs. "I'm bored."

I motion for him to come inside. He trips on the sash and tumbles to the floor, landing on his fat head.

"I thought you didn't want to wake Indy."

"You could have helped."

I grin. "Where's the fun in that?"

"Did I hear you playing?"

"You suck at subtle."

He shrugs. "Who said I was being subtle?" He sits on the floor with his back against the bed. "Go on. Play it for me."

"No interruptions," I order as I sit down and strum my guitar.

I've learned from my mistakes,

I've grown,

And I'll fight for your love,

I've always known,

You're the one I need,

The missing piece of me,

I'm determined to make you see.

I'm gonna win you back,

Prove my love is sincere,

Every moment,

I'll treasure and protect,

With you, I'll resurrect.

"What do you think?" I ask when I finish.

Gibson peeks into the window. "What happened to the old song?" he asks and begins to sing – off-key.

Oh, the one who slipped through my fingers,

Leaving trails of longing that still lingers,

She's the one I'll cherish through the night and day,

My love for her will never fade away.

I hate that song. It represents the past. How I let Indy go. How I was planning to live my life without her.

No more. I'm winning her back. Which is what the new song is about. But I'm not discussing my love life with these jokers.

"Did you bring the whole band with you?" I ask Dylan.

"Duh. It's no fun breaking into a house on my own."

Gibson climbs in the window followed by Jett. Fender brings up the rear.

"I don't know why we have to climb through the window," Fender complains as he shuts the window behind him.

Jett elbows him. "Where's your sense of adventure?"

"Not all of us are adrenaline junkies."

"I prefer the term adrenaline aficionado. Has a nice ring to it." He smiles before lifting up a bag I didn't notice he was carrying with him. "I brought beer."

"And I brought snacks," Gibson adds.

I groan. "You guys realize we're old enough to go to bars now. We don't need to have picnics in our bedrooms anymore."

When we were still struggling to get gigs and living off minimum wage, we'd gather in Dylan's bedroom of his apartment. We'd play music, eat junk food, drink beer, and talk about all the money we'd have when we were big rockstars.

Until his roommate would bang on the wall and threaten to call the cops on us. Trust me. It's not easy to flee from the cops when you're carrying a guitar while trying to make sure Jett doesn't pull down his pants and moon the 'pigs'.

"What do we think of Cash's new song?" Dylan asks once everyone is sitting on the floor with a beer and the bag of chips open in front of us.

"It's good," Gibson says.

"I can rock to it," Jett adds.

"Does this mean you're finally going to pull your head out of your ass and get your girl back?" Fender asks.

There's no denying it. They know me too well. "Yep."

Jett groans. "We're going to end up staying in Winter Falls forever."

"What's wrong?" Gibson taunts. "Worried you'll run out of women to trick into sleeping with you?"

"I don't have to trick them. With one glance at this man, they're in." Jett winks.

"If you want to win Indigo back, you're going to have to tell her why you left," Dylan says.

"Not happening."

"Tell her you're an idiot who made a mistake," Fender suggests.

Dylan snorts. "Indigo knows better. She knows you're not telling her the truth."

I groan. It's true. She does. But I will do everything in my power to prevent her from learning the truth. Because the truth will destroy her. And it's my job to protect her.

"Drop it," I growl at Dylan. "The truth will only hurt her."

He studies me for a second before nodding. "Okay then. We're back in the recording studio tomorrow since Cash has his muse back."

He's teasing me but I let it slide since he's not wrong. Indy is my muse. She's my everything.

Chapter 16

Not happening – Words guaranteed to get you in trouble no matter the context

Indigo

I stumble into the kitchen the next morning. I can barely keep my eyes open. I was up way too late last night mulling over what I overheard Cash say.

I shouldn't have eavesdropped but when he sings and plays his guitar, I can't resist. His smoky voice always reels me in. And the lyrics? Oh boy. His kiss brought me to my knees, but those lyrics cracked the wall around my heart.

And I'll fight for your love,
I've always known,
You're the one I need,
The missing piece of me,

I was ready to march into the room and finish up what we started on the sofa, but then he muttered those words 'not happening'. He doesn't ever plan to tell me the truth about why he broke my heart. Those cracks in my wall healed right up.

"Good morning, Indigo!" Dylan greets.

"What are you doing here?" I scan the kitchen. Dylan isn't the only guest this morning. "What are all of you doing here?"

I ask as if I hadn't heard them all climb into Cash's bedroom last night. Which is why I'm already dressed and not wearing my PJs. Who wants to bump into a famous rock band in her kitchen while wearing her kitty pajamas? Not this girl.

Gibson smirks. "We had a slumber party."

Fender grunts. "We fell asleep working on a song."

Jett sticks his tongue out at Fender. "Where's your sense of adventure?"

"I think you have enough adventure in you for the two of us."

Gibson smiles. "I have a sense of adventure."

The back door opens and Cash strolls in carrying several bags. "Getting take-out in this town is a hassle," he mutters before he notices me.

"Good morning, Indy." He nods toward his band mates. "Sorry about these ruffians. They climbed through my window last night and wouldn't leave."

"Says the man who ate all the potato chips," Dylan murmurs.

Cash ignores him and lifts up the bags he's carrying. "I brought breakfast as a peace offering."

"Yes!" Gibson dives at the bags.

Jett snatches a bag from Gibson's hands. "I'm starving."

Cash snaps his teeth at them. "If you ruin Indy's blueberry pancakes, I'm going to kick your asses."

My stomach rumbles. "Blueberry pancakes?"

Cash hands me a plate. "I remember they're your favorite."

Dang it! He's not supposed to remember my favorite breakfast food. And he definitely shouldn't be looking into my eyes with warmth in his. I focus on my plate.

"Thanks," I mutter.

Everyone settles around the kitchen table to dig into their food. The blueberry pancakes are fluffy and delicious. I bite my tongue to stop myself from moaning. But when my gaze meets Cash's across the table, his smirk tells me he knows.

"Are you guys going to the recording studio this morning?"

"Nope," Cash says. "Not until this afternoon. If it's okay with you, I want to help you bring those boxes to the library first."

If it's okay with me? Someone's a quick study.

"You don't have to. If you need to work, I understand."

"I'll help, too," Dylan volunteers. "We'll be done in no time and then we can record our new song. Ouch!" he yelps before glaring at Cash. "Why did you kick me?"

"No reason," Cash grumbles.

"It's no secret our *new* album will have *new* songs on it."

"Oh no," Gibson whines. "Mommy and Daddy are fighting."

Fender punches his shoulder. "No."

Gibson bats his eyelashes. "No, what?"

Fender doesn't respond. He simply grunts before returning his attention to his sausage and eggs.

Jett drops his fork and leans back against his chest while rubbing his stomach. "I guess I'll have to figure out a way to amuse myself while Cash and Dylan help Indigo."

I wave my fork at him. "No."

His eyes widen. "No what?"

"Don't act all innocent with me. You have troublemaker written all over you."

He bows. "Thank you. Thank you very much."

"It wasn't a compliment, dork."

His mouth gapes open. "Did she seriously call me a dork? Did anyone else hear her? Am I hallucinating again?"

Gibson groans. "You haven't been eating those mushrooms again, have you?"

"One time. One time I tried a mushroom."

"One time was enough," Fender grumbles.

"He was completely out of his mind," Dylan begins. "He bumped into a chair on the van and became convinced his leg was bleeding. So, he removed all his clothes."

"Including his underwear," Fender interrupts to add.

"He's running around the tour bus stark naked screaming about bleeding to death," Dylan continues. "Except there is no blood. We're literally driving down the highway with this lunatic screaming loud enough to be heard over Fender's bass solo during a concert."

"Lunatic is such a strong word," Jett complains.

"At some point, he decides he has to get off the bus because the bus is now poisoning him," Cash says. "What does the lunatic do?"

"Hey! I'm not a lunatic," Jett claims.

Cash rolls his eyes. "He tried to jump off the bus."

"We're driving sixty miles per hour and he's banging at the door to let him out before his blood turns green and his dick falls off," Dylan says.

"Good thing the bus doors don't open while the bus is driving," Fender grumbles.

"And now you know why Jett is not allowed to take hallucinogens again," Gibson concludes.

Jett sniffs. "If I want to try another hallucinogen, I will."

Gibson wiggles his phone at Jet. "And I'll phone Aurora to let her know."

Jett's eyes narrow. "You wouldn't."

"I totally would and you know it."

"Who's Aurora?" I ask.

"Jett's fantasy girlfriend," Gibson says.

"She is not my fantasy girlfriend. She's a shrew."

Dylan rolls his eyes. "She's the band's PA."

"Really? Why isn't she in Winter Falls?"

Jett wags his finger at me. "Don't you start, too."

Everyone laughs while Jett pushes to his feet and storms out of the room.

"Don't be a big baby," Gibson hollers after him.

I stand to gather our dishes and notice the time. "Shoot. I promised the librarian I'd be at the library by now."

"Gibson and I'll clean up," Fender says.

"Why did I get roped into helping?" Gibson complains but he winks as he takes the dishes from my hands.

I stare down at the boxes in the hallway. "We're going to need all morning to carry these boxes to the library."

Cash jingles a set of keys. "Good thing I borrowed a truck."

"A truck? From whom?"

He picks up two boxes and carries them toward the door. What he doesn't do is answer me. Which is an answer in and of itself. It must be one of his brother's trucks. Good. He's getting along with them. I may be protecting my own heart from Cash, but I want him to have the family he's always dreamed of.

Between Cash, Dylan, and me we have the truck loaded up in no time.

"Do you know the way?" I ask when we're settled in the truck.

"It's on the town square," Cash answers.

"How do you know?"

"The recording studio is two doors down from the square."

Ah. Makes sense.

Once we're parked in the square, I jump out and hurry to the library to meet the librarian. An elderly woman is at the check-out desk when I enter. Her gray hair is up in a bun held together with two pencils and she's wearing a brown cardigan. She has to be the librarian.

"You must be Gracious."

"Keep your voice down," is her response.

Oh boy. She doesn't merely resemble an old-fashioned librarian, she is one.

"Sorry," I whisper. "I phoned yesterday about donating some books."

Before she has a chance to answer, the door to the library flies open and Cash and Dylan saunter in carrying two boxes each. She scowls at them.

"Wipe your feet."

I bite my tongue before I remind her about the whole 'keeping your voice down' rule.

"Where should we put the boxes?"

She purses her lips at me before pointing toward a hallway. "In the storage room, I'll send Virginia your way to help you."

"Thank you."

I motion to the guys to follow me to the door marked 'storage'. "Set them here," I say.

They set the boxes where I indicate before leaving for the next load.

"One more load," Cash announces after the second trip. "Be right back."

"Sorry, sorry," a woman says as she bustles into the room. "I was working on the computer."

I smile at her but my smile freezes when I recognize her. "Virginia? Virginia Hale?"

She stares at me for a few seconds before recognition lights her eyes. "Indigo?"

"In the flesh," I say before hugging her.

When I pull away, she asks, "What are you doing here?"

"I could ask you the same thing."

"I asked first."

I bark out a laugh. Virginia is a shy thing but once you get to know her, she speaks her mind.

"My grandmother is from Winter Falls. Or, rather, was. She died."

"I'm sorry. I didn't realize."

I wave away her concern. "It's okay." I inhale a deep breath. "Or it will be."

Cash and Dylan saunter into the room.

"Look who I found, Cash. You remember my friend Virginia?"

Dylan glances over. His gaze catches on Virginia and he grins. He also forgets to pay attention to what's in front of him and runs straight into the wall. The boxes topple to his feet as books scatter everywhere.

"What's going on back there?" Gracious yells.

"Nothing!" Virginia yells back.

"Keep your voice down!"

Virginia rolls her eyes. "You better get out of here. Gracious is going to be a bear with all this ruckus."

Cash wipes his hands on his jeans. "We're finished anyway. Good seeing you, Virginia." He winks at her before strolling toward the door. "You coming with, butterfingers?"

"I-I-I-..." Dylan clears his throat. "Yeah, I'm coming."

He follows Cash out the door but can't help himself from glancing back at Virginia several times. I don't blame him. My friend is beautiful in an unassuming way.

I chuckle at his antics but Virginia scowls at him.

"I'll get out of your hair, but let's get together soon to catch up. I want to hear all about how you ended up in Winter Falls of all places."

I give her a quick hug before joining Cash and Dylan outside.

My year in Winter Falls is looking up. I glance at Cash and my body warms. No, not because of him. I hope I'm not lying.

Chapter 17

Goofballs – Surprisingly good support during a funeral

Indigo

I stare at the black dress on the bed. I don't want to put it on. If I do, it'll be real. Grandma's funeral will happen. And she'll be gone forever. What I wouldn't do to hear her voice one more time.

"Indy." Cash knocks on the door. "We need to get going if we don't want to be late."

My chest tightens and my hands shake. "J-j-just a minute." My words end on a sob.

"I'm coming in," he announces before opening the door.

He smiles at me and I break. "I don't want to go."

He gathers me into his arms before sitting on the bed. I burrow into him.

"Shhhh, sweetness," he murmurs as he rubs a hand up and down my back. I want to stay here in the comfort of his arms.

"We're here!" someone shouts from downstairs.

"Who is it?" I ask Cash.

"The band."

I lean back in his arms to view his face. "The band?"

He wipes the tears on my cheeks away. "Yeah, the band. They're my family so they're here to support you."

"Support me?"

"Because you're my family, too, Indy. You'll always be my family."

I should probably push him away, deny his words, but I can't. Not today. For today and today only I'm going to accept his comfort.

He rests his forehead against mine. "Are you ready?"

I snort. "Um, no. I'm wearing a robe and my face is all puffy from crying. I don't want to know how my make-up looks."

He kisses my nose. "You're always beautiful. Even snot-faced."

I slap his shoulder. "I do not have snot on my face."

He places me on my feet. "You can do this, Indy girl. You can do anything."

"O-o-okay."

"I'll go make sure the guys behave. We'll wait for you downstairs." He slaps my behind on his way out. "Get moving."

"Hey!"

He winks. "You got this, Indy girl."

I inhale a deep breath. Yeah, I got this.

Fifteen minutes later I hurry downstairs and follow the noise to the kitchen. I screech to a halt at the vision in front of me. All of the band members are wearing suits. And they make suits look good.

"Whoa. I don't know if I can bring you guys with me to the funeral."

"Why? What's wrong?" Dylan asks.

I motion toward them. "You're going to make the women of Winter Falls pop their ovaries."

Gibson winks. "Mission accomplished."

Jett pulls at his tie. "I feel constrained. Can you get claustrophobia from wearing a tie?"

"Baby," Fender grunts.

"No fighting at Indy's grandma's funeral," Cash orders.

"It would liven things up," Jett claims.

"Shall we get going?" I ask before Jett can concoct some plan to 'liven things up'. I do not want to know what those words mean to him. The drummer should have the words 'caution daredevil' tattooed on his forehead.

Since cars are considered evil in Winter Falls, we pile into two golf carts and make our way to the cemetery for the funeral.

A crowd has already gathered in a circle around the plot where Grandma will be buried. Cash grasps my hand when we arrive and leads me to the front row reserved for family members. I glance around for Mom but I don't find her.

Mrs. West – the woman Grandma dictated should handle the funeral ceremony – stands and steps to the end of the grave. "Shall we begin?"

I panic. We can't begin before Mom arrives.

"We're here today—"

"Wait!" I shout. "Mom's not here."

Mrs. West smiles as she approaches me. "Do you know when Raven will be arriving?"

"Um…" I bite my lip. "No?"

She squeezes my hand. “Why don’t we wait a few minutes?”

“Please.”

“Of course.”

Once she’s gone, Cash hauls me close. “Have you spoken to your mom?”

“I sent her a few messages but she hasn’t responded.”

He frowns. “Is this normal?”

I sigh. “Lately, yes. We mostly communicate via my dad.”

“Why don’t you ring him?”

I reach for my purse but panic when I realize I didn’t bring one. “I didn’t bring my phone.”

“Here.” He digs his phone out of his pocket.

I murmur my thanks and walk off to find some privacy. I try Mom first but she doesn’t pick up. No surprise there. Guess I’ll try Dad.

“Hey, baby girl,” Dad answers the phone.

“Hi, Dad. Do you know where Mom is?”

When he doesn’t immediately speak, I know his answer is going to anger me.

“She isn’t coming to Saffron’s funeral. I tried to convince her. I even booked our flights and rented a car.”

“But…”

“She refused to go and when I said I was going alone—”

“She threatened to divorce you,” I fill in since this isn’t the first time Mom has pulled that particular trick. It’s one of her favorites.

“I’m sorry, Indigo. I should have called her bluff.”

“It’s okay, Dad. I need to go.”

I hang up. I don't want to listen to his excuses for putting up with Mom. Not today. Besides, I know them all by heart.

"You okay, Indy?" Cash asks and I glance up to discover the band members have gathered around me.

"Mom's not coming."

He wraps me up in his arms. "I'm sorry, Indy girl."

"Who needs her?" Dylan asks. "You've got us."

"And we're way prettier to look at," Gibson declares.

"I'm the prettiest of them all," Jett declares and Fender slaps his palm in his face to push him away.

"I didn't know your band was delusional," I mock whisper to Cash.

"They grow on you. Like a fungus you can't get rid of."

Gibson sighs. "If I've told you once, I've told you a million times. If it hurts when you piss, go to the doctor."

"He would know." Jett winks.

Dylan grunts. "And now you know why we buy condoms in bulk."

"Excuse me." Mrs. West pushes her way through the circle toward me. "Did you reach Raven? Do you know when she'll arrive?"

"She's not coming." I usually don't have the urge to swear. Teaching small children for years has cured me of my potty mouth. But today there are some choice words I wouldn't mind voicing about dear old mom.

"I'm sorry, dear. Maybe we should begin."

"I'll be there in a moment."

She starts toward the crowd again but stops in front of Fender. "Oh my, you are a big boy, aren't you?"

He flashes her a smile and I nearly fall to my knees. Fender's a handsome man but when he smiles and flashes those dimples? Oh my. Those dimples should be classified as weapons of mass destruction. Able to wipe out a group of women with one flash.

"You're drooling," Cash snarls.

I pat his chest. "Don't be jealous. You're still my favorite member of the band."

"I know." He winks.

I straighten my back. "Let's do this."

Cash grasps my hand and leads me back to the burial spot with his band trailing after us.

I didn't expect his bandmates to show up today. But I'm glad they did. Their support – and goofiness – has made today bearable.

I sit on a chair in front of the hole in the ground. But today's not over yet.

Chapter 18

Skinny dipping – Two words you don't expect to be uttered at a funeral

CASH

I seethe as I sit next to Indy. Her mother is a bitch. How dare she not show up to her own mother's funeral? After everything I've done to ensure Indy and her mother maintain a relationship, she does this?

I've already decided to win Indy back. But, if I hadn't, I would be dead set on it now. Since there's apparently no reason to please Indy's mother anymore.

"Welcome," Mrs. West greets. "Welcome to Saffron's family." She nods to Indy who grips my hand hard enough I fear I won't be able to play the guitar for awhile.

"Welcome to Saffron's friends. And welcome to our special guests." Mrs. West winks at Fender whose cheeks darken until they're bright red.

"We are joined here by our memory, by our lives with Saffron, by our affection, and by our sorrow. Let us spend a few moments preparing our hearts."

Everyone bows their heads for a moment until she speaks again.

"Let us call for peace. May there be Peace in the East! May there be Peace in the South! May there be Peace in the West! May there be Peace in the North!"

"May there be Peace throughout the whole world," everyone answers.

This doesn't sound similar to the funeral for my mother. Although, that's probably for the better. Having two drug addicts argue about a man they don't want to share is not the memory I want Indy to have of her grandma's funeral.

"We meet here today in both sadness and joy to bid a fond farewell to Saffron, a much loved member of our community. We are sad because a chapter has closed. Yet we should be joyful by the closing for allowing a new chapter to begin."

Mrs. West smiles at the people gathered. "I now invite you to share memories of Saffron. Indigo?"

I help Indy stand and ensure her feet are steady before leading her to Mrs. West. I take a place behind her as she opens up a tattered piece of paper.

"Um… Hi. I'm Indigo. Saffron's granddaughter." She inhales a deep breath. "Grandma requested I share my favorite memory of her today. And by requested, I mean she ordered me."

When everyone laughs, Indy's shoulders release some tension.

"It's hard to pick a favorite memory of Grandma. There are so many." She pauses. "But this memory always brings a smile to my face and since I could use a smile today..." She clears her throat.

"About a month after Grandpa died, Grandma contacted me. She said I needed to get my rear end to Winter Falls post haste. I came as quick as I could. I was convinced Grandma was sick and dying. I was so worried, I was hyperventilating on the plane. They upgraded me to first class because I was scaring the other passengers. I spent my one and only experience in first class breathing into a bag."

I'll fly her first class wherever she wants to go. No hyperventilating required.

"Anyway, I arrived in Winter Falls to find Grandma perfectly fine. In fact, she was excited. She had 'requested my presence' because now that her old man was dead, she was getting a tattoo. And she needed a ride."

Saffron had a tattoo? I wish I had met the woman.

"I yelled at Grandma for a good five minutes for scaring me. Her response? Quit your yapping or we'll miss my appointment. Grandma was the most stubborn woman I knew."

It must be hereditary since Indy's the most stubborn woman I know.

"I drove her to White Bridge to her appointment. When we entered the tattoo parlor and it was full of rough looking men with long hair, I thought Grandma's eyes were going to explode. You know how Grandma loved long hair on men."

"Damn straight!" An elderly man with long hair shouts.

"To make a long story short, Grandma got her tattoo and we ended up at lunch with a bunch of bikers at a biker bar.

Grandma's smile was so big, I worried her dentures would fall out. She played *All Right Now* on the jukebox and forced every single rough around the edges biker in the bar to dance with her. I sucked down the Shirley Temples she kept ordering her 'little girl' while she guzzled beer."

A man flashes the devil ears. "Rock on, Saffron!"

"It was all fun and games until she asked one of the men if he wanted to do a body shot. Then, I was done and hauled her out of there. She never failed to complain about me ruining her fun at the biker bar every time we spoke since."

There are claps and cheers as Indy finishes her speech. I escort her back to her spot.

"Your grandma was the shit," Dylan says.

"Where's this biker bar?" Jett asks.

Fender grunts. "Do not tell him."

"Would anyone else like to share a story about Saffron?" Mrs. West asks.

"I'm next!" Sage yells. The five ladies who comprise the gossip gals make their way to the front of the crowd.

"Saffron was a good friend of ours," Sage says.

"Despite not approving of the term gossip gals," Feather adds.

Clove snorts. "Saffron was the biggest gossip of them all."

"Are you going to share a memory of Saffron with us?" Mrs. West asks.

Sage purses her lips. "Don't get your panties in a twist just because we didn't accept your application to become a gossip gal."

Mrs. West cocks her eyebrow. "This is a funeral."

Cayenne rolls her eyes. "We're aware. We're old, not senile."

"We had a difficult time coming up with one story to share," Sage begins, "but we finally decided on our skinny-dipping accident."

A man wearing a police uniform behind me groans.

Sage points a finger at him. "No lip from you, young man. Skinny dipping is not illegal."

Jett perks up. "It's not? Where's the fun if it's legal?"

Gibson elbows him. "Are you feeling okay? Being naked with a bunch of women isn't fun for you anymore?"

Indy leans over to whisper in my ear, "Bunch of women?"

"You don't want to know."

"We didn't plan to go skinny dipping," Petal declares.

"But someone washed our pink sweatshirts with fabric softener." Sage glares at Clove.

"It's not my fault," Clove huffs. "Sirius did the laundry."

"Instead of making our sweatshirts soft, they were itchy. Real itchy," Cayenne explains.

"Which is why we took them off."

"You didn't have to remove your bras," the policeman behind me says.

"Of course, we did," Sage declares. "Once we decided to swim in the river to relieve the itch, we needed to remove all our clothes."

"What does this story have to do with Saffron?" Mrs. West asks.

"Saffron happened upon us swimming in the river and decided to join in," Feather says.

Indy groans and covers her face with her hands.

Petal giggles. "She did the best cannonballs."

"But then the chief of police came and ruined our fun." Sage glares at the man behind me.

"You shouldn't have been playing hide and seek when the high school biology class was on a field trip to gather wild herbs," he responds.

Clove fists her hands at her hips. "How the heck were we supposed to know the high school biology class was in the woods?"

Mrs. West purses her lips at Clove. "Maybe you didn't know but you didn't have to jump out of the bushes while you were stark naked and shout peekaboo at them. Poor Kai peed his pants in fright. He's still afraid to go into the woods."

"That's not my fault. If his mother weren't such a prude, he wouldn't be scared to see a pair of boobs in real life."

"This town is awesome," Gibson whispers.

Jett nods in agreement. "I'm never leaving here."

"Thank you for your contribution, ladies." Mrs. West herds the women away.

"Thank you for attending Saffron's remembrance. The usual manner to end our gathering is to offer food and drink to the deceased. Saffron requested for everyone to meet at the diner to enjoy a celebratory meal in her honor."

"There's food?" Fender marches off in the direction of town. Gibson and Jett hurry after him.

"Do you want to stay here awhile?" I ask Indy once everyone has left and we're alone.

"Can't. According to Grandma's very detailed instructions, I should be at the diner to welcome everyone."

I stand and offer her my hand. "Your chariot awaits."

"I thought today would be sad, but it hasn't been. It's the celebration of her life Grandma wanted."

Good. I've had enough of Indy's tears to last a lifetime. I'll hold her whenever she cries but I don't want her to cry ever again. Her tears slay me.

Chapter 19

Mistake – Depends on your perspective

CASH

Indy yawns as she climbs the stairs to the house.

"What a day," she mumbles.

"I've never been to a funeral with karaoke before."

She giggles as she opens the door. "I can't believe you got into a fight at my grandma's funeral."

"It's not my fault," I pout as I follow her inside.

She raises her eyebrows. "Really? It's not *your* fault. It wasn't *your* fault when you claimed the gossip gals were cheating?"

"They were cheating."

"Of course, they were. They're the gossip gals."

"I didn't realize being a gossip gal meant you get to cheat at karaoke."

"Poor Cash." She pats my arm. "Wasn't voted the best singer at Grandma's funeral."

I growl. "I am the best singer."

She rolls her eyes but before she has a chance to speak her phone beeps. She picks it up from the kitchen table where she left it this morning. She scowls as she reads the message.

"I cannot believe her." She slams the phone down on the table. "Does Mom seriously think I don't realize she's lying? What a bitch."

Her eyes widen and she slaps her hands over her mouth. I start to joke about Indy having a potty mouth but then I notice the tears welling in her eyes. Shit.

"Hey, now, Indy girl." I pry her hands from her mouth before framing her face with my hands. "It's okay to lash out sometimes." When she doesn't speak, I push her. "What did Raven say?"

"Mom said it's not true she threatened to divorce Dad if he came today. We buried her mother today and all she's worried about is whether I love Dad more than her."

I grit my teeth and clamp my mouth shut. I'm afraid if I open my mouth, I'll tell Indy the truth about her mom. The truth that will hurt her. But I'm done hurting Indy.

I rub circles on Indy's skin with my thumbs until my anger is under control. "She can argue all she wants. We both know you prefer me over the two of them."

I'm joking but Indy's eyes flare with heat. I want to throw her over my shoulder and carry her to her bedroom where I can remind her of how much she likes me. Of how good I can make her feel. Of how I can make her forget the world outside of the two of us.

"I think I do," she murmurs.

Nothing can stop me now. I slam my mouth down on hers. At the first hint of her candy mixed with wicked taste, I groan.

I've missed her taste. I've missed her in my arms. I've plain missed her.

She threads her fingers through my hair and tugs me closer. I'll come as close as you want, Indy girl. As close as I can be.

I prowl forward until her back is against the wall. I press my hard length into her stomach and she mewls in response. I don't want a little mewl. I want her writhing beneath me, begging for relief.

I grasp her knee and hitch her leg around my waist. I thrust against her core and she arches her back forcing her breasts into my chest. This is more like it. I thrust against her again and she wraps her other leg around me. *Yes.*

I release her lips to nibble along her jaw. She lifts her chin to give me room to maneuver. I bite and nip at her neck and she grinds against my hard length. Searching for relief. She's not getting relief while we're both fully clothed. Not on my watch.

"Why don't we take this to the bedroom?" I whisper into her ear.

"I want you. I don't care if this is a mistake."

"This isn't a mistake," I growl.

I carry her to her bedroom and deposit her on the bed before laying on top of her. "Tell me you realize this isn't a mistake," I demand.

Her legs wrap around my waist and she begins rubbing herself up and down my cock. "Don't care if it's a mistake," she gasps out.

I grasp her hips to stop her movement. "Promise you won't regret this in the morning."

"I promise."

I search her hazel eyes for the truth but all I see is desire.

"I'm holding you to your promise."

"Are you going to ravish me or talk all night?"

Fuck it. I'm done discussing whether she'll regret this. She's a grown ass woman. If she says she won't regret being with me, I need to trust that she's being honest with me.

"Arms up."

She immediately lifts her arms. I kneel and trail my hands along her legs until I reach the hem of her dress. I draw the fabric up but freeze when I touch skin. I glance down and groan at the vision before me.

"Thigh highs? You're wearing thigh highs?"

"It's too cold outside for bare legs," she claims as she bats her eyelashes. She knows exactly how sexy I think thigh highs are.

I tap the bow at the top of the thigh high. "I'm going to fuck you with these on."

"Yes, please."

I grunt. "You're a tease."

She wiggles her fingers. "You're the one who promised to fuck me but is frozen in place."

I close my eyes as all the blood in my body rushes to my cock. Indy loses all her prim and proper in bed. It's the sexiest thing I've ever experienced. I'm addicted.

I whip the dress off her and throw it over my shoulder. The sight of Indy beneath me nearly has me coming in my pants. She's wearing a black lace bra through which her nipples are visible and matching lace panties. Add in the thigh highs and she's the sexiest thing I've ever seen.

"Are you trying to kill me?"

She giggles. The sound fills me with happiness. I want to hear her giggle while we're fooling around in bed every day for the rest of our lives. I'm certain when we're old and gray, I'll still want her. She's a temptress and I have no desire to fight her pull.

"Maybe." She bats her eyelashes.

Two can play at this game. I tug her bra cup down and her breast pops out. I latch onto her nipple. Her back arches off the bed as she moans. While I suck on one nipple, I knead and pinch her other breast until she's writhing beneath me.

She wraps her legs around my waist and grounds her center on my cock. Her breath hitches and I realize she's about to come. Not until I'm inside her.

I release her breasts and kneel. She pounds her fist on the mattress. "Why did you stop? You tease!"

"Don't worry, sweetness. We're just getting started."

I trail a finger down her chest to her panties. "Are you wet for me?"

Her legs fall open and she spreads them wide. "Why don't you find out for yourself?"

It's an invitation I can't resist. I dive into her panties. I ignore her clit to sink two fingers into her. She pulses around me.

"You're soaked."

Her cheeks darken but she doesn't shy away from my words. "It's what happens when you tease me."

I pump my fingers in and out of her and watch as her head falls back and her mouth opens in a silent gasp.

"Do you want to come all over my fingers?"

Her eyes flutter open. "No. I want you."

"Correct answer." I pull out my fingers and lift them to my mouth. Her eyes flare as she watches me lick her excitement from my fingers. "As sweet as I remember."

She reaches for my pants and unbuckles my belt before snapping the button open. She pulls the zipper down and my cock flops out into her hands. She wraps a hand around me and pumps.

My eyes close as I concentrate on how good it feels to have her hand on me. She knows exactly how tight to hold me. How to twist at the exact right moment. This woman knows me. She's perfect for me.

When she cradles my balls in her hands, I'm done. I'm not coming in her hand. I plan to be buried deep inside her when I come.

I remove a condom from the wallet in my back pocket before batting her hands away. She smirks as she lifts her hands above her causing her breasts to jut forward. She knows exactly what she's doing to me and she's enjoying it. The little minx.

I make quick work of sheathing my cock before pulling her panties down her legs.

"Widen your legs for me."

Indy doesn't hesitate to follow my orders and I fit my hips between her thighs before notching my cock at her entrance.

"You sure?"

She glares at me. "Are you kidding me? You're asking me now if I'm—"

Her words are cut off with a gasp as I thrust into her until I'm buried to the hilt. Her walls pulse around me and I grit my teeth before I come. She's coming first if it kills me.

"Move," she orders.

I slowly withdraw before plunging into her again. She wraps her legs around me and together we find our rhythm. She meets my every thrust with a lift of her hips.

I blanket her with my body and bury my head in her neck. I inhale her strawberry scent and her fingers dig into my shoulders as we move together. The sound of skin slapping against skin fills the room.

This is it. My favorite thing in the world. Not making music. Not screaming fans. This. Buried deep inside the woman I love.

It's not long before her walls tighten around me.

"Are you going to come for me, sweetness?"

I don't wait for her response before slinking a hand between us to find her clit. I barely have a chance to touch her before she goes off.

"Yes!" she shouts.

"Say my name," I demand as I rub her clit to prolong her climax.

"Cash. Cash. Cash," she chants.

I increase my pace until I lose all rhythm and find my own climax.

"Indy," I growl as I come.

I continue to pump into her until I'm completely drained. I collapse on top of her but quickly roll to the side.

"This is only the beginning," I tell her.

I'm surprised she doesn't respond, but when I glance over at her. She's asleep.

I chuckle as I gather her in my arms. Tomorrow we'll discuss where this relationship is going.

Chapter 20

Trouble – You know you stepped in it when a rockstar chases after you down the street in his boxer shorts

Indigo

I wake slowly. I must have forgotten to turn down the heat last night because it's nice and warm in bed this morning. I snuggle into my blankets. I don't need to be anywhere this morning. Might as well enjoy the warmth while I can.

Hold on. This isn't a blanket behind me. It's a naked body. A hard, naked body. I lift the blanket and glance down at myself. Where are my clothes? What in the world?

The memories crash into me. Cash hovering over me as he moved inside me. The look of ecstasy on his face when he climaxed. Me begging him to fuck me.

Ugh. I'm an idiot. How am I supposed to keep Cash out of my heart when I let him into my body? Stupid. Stupid. Stupid.

Meow.

Katy Purry stares up at me from her spot on the floor. She cocks her head and I swear her eyebrows lift in condemnation.

I wag a finger at her. "Don't you start with me."

Cash groans and rolls away from me. Perfect. Without his arm draped over my waist, I can sneak out and he'll be none the wiser. I lift the blankets and scooch out of bed.

I dress as fast as I can before escaping the bedroom. Once I've taken care of business in the bathroom, I follow my kitty to the kitchen to feed her.

"What am I going to do?" I ask her.

She doesn't respond as she continues to devour her breakfast.

"How am I going to face him? We have to live in this house together until he finishes the album."

I groan and bury my face in my hands. Why did I ever agree to let him stay here? Stupid lease agreement. Who was I kidding thinking I could keep my hands off of him? The man is irresistible. There's only one way to resist him. Keep my distance.

Perfect plan. I'll make myself scarce whenever he's around. Starting with now. I march to the front door. But when I open it, Katy Purry protests.

"Shush, kitty."

She doesn't shush. In fact, she gets louder.

"You can't come with, you little terror."

The floor creaks above me. Oh no. Cash is awake. I need to get out of here now.

"Sorry, kitty."

I hold her back with my foot while I sneak out the door.

"Indy!"

In response to Cash's yell, I increase my pace until I'm speed walking down the sidewalk toward Main Street. I nod at a woman as I pass her. She tugs on a leash and I smile down at her… goat? She's walking a goat on a leash? I rub my eyes to clear them but there's still a goat on the sidewalk.

"Come on, Pan. I promise we won't go to my sister's house."

Baa!

"I didn't mean Juniper. I know you love Juniper more than you love me."

Baa!

"I'm not trying to guilt trip you."

I place a hand over my mouth to stop my giggle from escaping.

The woman sighs. "Go ahead and laugh."

"I'm not trying to make fun of you but you're seriously having a discussion with a goat."

"Because someone's not listening." She glares at the goat before addressing me. "I'm Gabrielle."

"Hi, I'm—

"You're Indigo, Saffron's granddaughter."

How does she know? Oh yeah. "Winter Falls."

She beams at me. "Isn't it great? I wish I'd grown up here instead of Saint Louis."

"Indy!"

At Cash's shout, I scan the area but there isn't anywhere to hide.

"Oh my!" Gabrielle fans her face. "I wish I could get my man to chase after me in nothing but his boxers."

"Please tell me he isn't coming this way."

She laughs. "You're in big trouble."

She doesn't know the half of it.

Cash grasps my hand and whirls me around. "Why are you avoiding me?"

"I'm not avoiding you."

Gabrielle barks out a laugh behind me. "This is awesome. I'm going to win a bet for a change."

Cash ignores her. "You promised you wouldn't regret it in the morning."

"I also said it was a mistake."

"Us having sex was not a mistake," he growls.

I gasp. "It's not bad enough you're strutting around outside in your boxer shorts? You're just going to announce we had sex to the whole world?"

"I don't fucking care. The whole world can know how much I want you."

I yank my hand away from his and plant my fists on my hips. "Really? You want me so much you couldn't wait to get rid of me at graduation."

He runs a hand through his hair. "It was for your own good."

"My own good?" I poke him in the chest. "You broke my heart for my own good?"

"Yes."

"Really? You didn't break up with me so you could pursue your dream of becoming a rockstar without me? So you could sleep with all the groupies and not worry about cheating on your boring old high school girlfriend?"

He reaches for my hands but I slap him away. "You're not boring and I didn't break up with you to become a rockstar."

I throw my hands in the air. "Then, why did you?"

He frowns. What he doesn't do is answer me.

"And you wonder why I called last night a mistake."

I stomp away but Cash grasps my bicep to stop me. I glare at him. "I did not give you permission to touch me, Mr. Evans."

He drops his hand. "I'm sorry. Please don't go."

I snort. "You have got to be kidding me. You know what happened when I begged you not to leave me? When I begged you to let me fix whatever was wrong between us?" I lean close to hiss in his face. "You left. Walked away without looking back."

Gabrielle clears her throat. "As much as I'm enjoying this – and I am truly enjoying this – I think you may want to relocate your conversation to somewhere private." She nods toward the group of elderly women on the sidewalk across the street. "The gossip gals won't hesitate to listen to everything and then post the entire conversation on the Winter Falls Facebook page word for word."

"Works for me. I'm done with this conversation anyway." I stomp away.

"I'll tell you," Cash calls.

I halt.

"I'll tell you everything."

I glance at him over my shoulder.

"If you promise not to be mad."

"Dude." Gabrielle snorts. "That ship has sailed and is halfway across the ocean already."

Baa!

"Pan agrees."

"Fine," Cash says. "I'll tell you everything and you can get as mad as you want because the goat said you could."

I'm frozen on the sidewalk. I want to know why Cash dumped me at our high school graduation. But I don't want to want to know. I want to be able to walk away and forget all about him.

Because that tactic has worked so well for me over the past eleven years.

"Fine," I huff and march toward the house. "But I'm not promising I won't sic Katy Purry on you."

"You're mean," Cash declares but there's no heat in his words. In fact, he's grinning.

He thinks he's won this round. I narrow my eyes on him. He hasn't won a thing. Jerk.

Chapter 21

The truth – Won't always set you free but it will make you really, really mad

CASH

I follow Indy as she stomps into the house. It probably makes me an asshole but I can't resist staring at her ass. An ass I dug my hands into last night as I plunged into her body. I want to do it again and again but after this conversation, I'll be lucky if she'll let me near her again let alone touch her naked skin.

She flings the door open and I cough to stop from grinning. Indy is adorable when she's angry.

She whirls around on me with her hazel eyes flaring. "Well?"

Crap. Why the hell did I agree to tell her the truth? This is going to be a disaster.

I clear my throat. "Can we sit down?"

"Nope." She points to the floor in front of my feet. "You're going to stand right there and explain why you dumped me in front of the entire high school on graduation day."

I rub a hand down my face as I stall. "You were too good for me."

"Asshole."

Uh oh. She's swearing. And we're not in bed where her swearing causes my blood to heat.

"I'm the one." She stabs her chest with a finger. "I'm the only one who decides if you're good enough for me or not. I gave you my virginity. Does that say he's not good enough for me?"

"I don't want to hurt you."

She rears back. "You don't want to hurt me? It was okay to hurt me eleven years ago but all of a sudden you've grown a conscience and don't want to hurt me anymore?"

"I never wanted to hurt you. I…" I cut myself off before I admit how much I love her, how much I've always loved her.

She crosses her arms over her chest and taps her foot. "You what?"

"Can't we let bygones be bygones?"

I'm surprised I don't turn to ice considering how cold her gaze on me is.

"Let bygones be bygones?"

"I—"

"No!" She cuts me off. "I'm speaking now." I motion for her to continue but she doesn't need my permission. "If you want to let bygones be bygones, get out." She motions to the door. "Get the heck out and never come back. Never show your face to me again."

"But I'm in Winter Falls to record my album."

Damn. Do I sound as lame as I think?

She leans close to me and hisses, "I don't care." She begins to walk off. "I knew you wouldn't tell me the truth."

"I did tell you the truth. I'm not good enough for you."

"True but you didn't break up with me because you're not good enough for me." She glances over her shoulder. "There's another reason you're not telling me."

I watch her hurry up the stairs. If I let her walk away now, it's over. I'll never get another chance with her. I don't want it to be over. I never want our relationship to be over.

"I don't want you to hate me."

She pauses. "Why would I hate you?"

"Because it's my fault your mom wasn't here yesterday for the funeral."

Her eyes widen. "Mom didn't come to Grandma's funeral because of you?"

"Yes."

"What did you do? Sleep with both of them?"

I grunt. "You're not funny."

"I'm hilarious." She clears her throat. "But seriously, what other reason could there possibly be for you to think you're the reason Mom was a no show yesterday? Mom didn't show because she's been fighting with Grandma for a decade."

"Because I was there."

Her brow wrinkles. "Because you were there? Mom didn't come to Winter Falls because you were here?"

I blow out a breath. "I think so."

"You need to explain yourself."

I should have never opened my mouth. This explanation is going to hurt Indy, which is the last thing I want to do.

"Can we at least sit down?"

Katy Purry races out of the hallway and down the stairs toward me. I cover my face with my hands. "Not the face."

Indy sighs. "Stop taunting Katy. She's perfectly harmless."

I drop my hands. "Really? Did you not notice today's present?"

She holds up a hand. "Stop. You can't distract me with your libelous accusations of my poor kitty."

I debate explaining the difference between libel and slander to her but realize I'm stalling again. If I don't want to get kicked out, stalling time's over. Shit.

"I need a coffee," I murmur as I trudge to the kitchen. I guess I'm not done stalling after all.

When Indy follows me, I blow out a breath in relief. I haven't lost her yet. I will soon. But not yet.

She sits at the table and I place a coffee in front of her before sitting across from her. I'd rather be close enough to touch her, but she won't want to ever touch me again after my confession.

"You may begin."

"Thank you, your highness."

"Stop stalling."

Fuck. Time to come clean. I don't want to, but she's going to learn the truth eventually anyway. I'm surprised her mom hasn't told her already.

"Your mom told me to end our relationship."

"What?" she gasps.

"Your mom visited me after school a few days before graduation. She told me I was ruining your life and if I didn't end our relationship, she wouldn't pay your college tuition."

Indy scowls. "You have got to be kidding me."

"I wish I was."

"And you listened to her?"

"Of course, I did."

She pounds her fist on the table. "My mother is such a freaking poop stain." She jumps to her feet and begins pacing the room. "I can't believe this. How dare she blackmail you? How dare she come between us?"

She blows out a breath and her initial anger drains from her. "All I've ever done is try to earn her love. I do everything she tells me to. I have the job she wants me to have. I date the men she wants me to date."

She sniffs and tears well in her eyes. "I can't believe I didn't visit Grandma for years because I wanted to please Mom and not incur her wrath."

I go to her. I can't stand it when she's in pain. "Don't beat yourself up. It's natural to want your mother to love you."

She huffs. "But she broke us apart. She broke my heart because she didn't want us together."

I palm her neck and lay my forehead against hers. "She was right. I wasn't good enough for you. I was the son of an alcoholic who never knew his dad. I was barely graduating high school."

She rears back. "Now you're just being an idiot."

"Excuse me?"

"You can't help who your parents are. None of us can. No matter how much we may wish otherwise." One lonely tear escapes and she swipes it away with the back of her hand.

"And who cares if you were barely graduating high school? Not everyone is book smart. You're a talented musician. I think talent outweighs book smarts every day of the week."

I smirk. "You think I'm talented."

"Don't you start flirting. You're not out of the doghouse yet."

"Woof!"

She ducks her head but not before I notice her smile. "Why didn't you tell me this at the time? Why did you break up with me?"

"Because I was an idiot eighteen-year-old who believed every word your mother said."

"Cash."

I shrug. "What? It's true."

"We're all idiots when we're teenagers, but you still should have told me."

"No way. I wasn't causing a rift between you and your mom. I didn't want you to lose your mother the way I lost mine."

"I'm not sure it'd be much of a loss," she mutters before raising her voice. "Cash, sweetie, it's not your job to protect me."

"It will always be my job to protect you."

"You should have told me."

"You can repeat yourself as many times as you want, but it doesn't change anything."

She frames my face with her hands. "Promise me."

"Anything."

Whatever she wants is hers. Unless she wants me to leave. That's not happening. I will never leave her again. Her mother can't influence me anymore. Especially after she was a no show yesterday.

"Promise me you'll always tell me the truth from now on."

"Will you forgive me if I do?"

She kisses my nose. "There's nothing to forgive. My mom's the one who should be begging for my forgiveness."

I ignore the mom comment. I don't want to discuss her mom anymore. "I promise I will always tell you the truth."

"Good. We can't build a relationship on a pack of lies."

My heart gallops in my chest. "Does this mean you want to be with me?"

She blows out a breath. "I'm probably making the biggest mistake of my life but I can't resist you."

"You don't have to."

She rolls her eyes. "Such a charmer."

"Only for you, Indy. Always for you."

She bites her bottom lip as she studies me. "But what about when you leave Winter Falls?"

I won't be going anywhere Indy isn't. But I keep those thoughts to myself. She'd freak out if she knew my plan was to keep her forever. She's not ready for my declarations of love and forever.

"You're not here forever either," I remind her.

"But I'm here for the next year."

"I guess it's going to take a year for *Cash & the Sinners* to write our next album."

She smacks my chest. "You can't put your career on hold for a year for me."

I waggle my eyebrows. "Wanna bet?"

"I'm serious. Your career is important."

"Not as important as you are."

She studies my face and I let her see it all. My love for her. My desire to never let her go. "You're not lying."

"Of course, I'm not lying. I just promised to always be truthful with you."

"You didn't leave me to become a big rockstar?"

"I told you I didn't."

"My mom guilted you into ending our relationship?"

I pull her close and wrap my arms around her. "I'm sorry, Indy. I didn't want to hurt you."

She buries her face in my shoulder. "You didn't hurt me. Mom did."

"Please don't let this cause a rift between you and your mom."

"That ship sailed when she didn't show up to Grandma's funeral."

I kiss her hair. "I'm sorry."

"I'm not. I'm glad Mom showed her true colors."

"Indy, don't lose your mother over this."

She squeezes my ass and my cock immediately perks up. He doesn't care how heavy the conversation is. He knows what he wants. And what he wants is in my arms.

"I'm done discussing this," Indy declares. "I think we have better things to do."

Before I have a chance to respond, she presses her lips against mine. I forget all about her mommy issues as Indy's tongue pushes into my mouth. I'll let her play for a minute before showing her who's in charge.

Who will always be in charge if I have my way. And I intend to have my way – and Indy – for the rest of my life.

Chapter 22

Jump in with both feet – Abandon all reason and proceed without caution

INDIGO

"I'm home," I shout as I enter the house.

"Cash?" I call when he doesn't respond. He must be in the recording studio. Bummer. I guess my exciting news will have to wait.

Time to get out of these interview clothes and into some sweatpants. I shrug off my good coat and drop my purse at the door before heading toward the stairs. Something crunches when I step on the first tread. It's a piece of paper. What is a piece of paper doing here?

Follow me. I read.

Follow me? In which direction? I scan the area and discover another piece of paper halfway up the stairs.

Moving up in the right direction.

I hurry up the rest of the stairs toward the hallway. There's an arrow leading toward my bedroom.

This way.

"Are you waiting in the bed with no clothes on? Corny."

But when I enter my bedroom, it's empty. I search the room and notice the window is open. My winter coat is folded over the ledge with my boots on the floor underneath.

Wear me.

I don the coat and shove my feet into the boots before sticking my head out the window.

"Cash?"

He doesn't respond but there's another arrow pointing to the roof.

"What if I'm afraid of heights?"

He peeks over the ledge. "You never used to be afraid of heights."

"I also used to be a dumb teenager."

"You were never dumb."

I roll my eyes. "Argue about how idiotic teenagers are later. Help me now."

He reaches down and I grab his hand before scrambling out of the window and onto the roof.

"You're lucky I didn't have to climb a tree," I grumble as I brush dirt off of my interview slacks.

"You never minded when I had to climb trees."

"Because I knew your inflated ego would cushion your fall if necessary."

He chuckles before leading me toward a blanket and helping me to sit.

"Champagne?"

I open my arms wide to indicate the great outdoors we're currently in. "Where are you going to get champagne?"

He motions to a picnic basket I hadn't noticed.

"We're having a picnic on the roof?"

"Remember when we used to spend hours sitting on the roof outside your window because your mom didn't like me."

I scowl at the mention of my mom. I'm still reeling from Cash's revelation of what she did. Of how she broke us apart. Mom has always tried to control me but blackmailing my boyfriend to dump me? She went too far.

But I don't want to think about Mom and how she doesn't love me no matter what I do when I'm alone with Cash.

"She was probably being overprotective of her little girl." I hate how my words sound as if I'm defending her.

Cash waggles his eyebrows. "I did deflower you."

"Deflower?" I giggle. "I don't remember there being any flowers."

"Because I'm an idiot. I should have given you flowers and taken you to a hotel for our first time."

I raise my eyebrows. "You didn't enjoy the flatbed of Dylan's truck?"

He groans. "I had rugburns on my knees for days."

I tap my chin. "Are they rugburns if there wasn't a rug?"

"Stop being a pain or there'll be no champagne for you."

I clasp my chest. "Oh no. No champagne. Whatever shall I do? I cannot drink the peasant's water."

"Smart ass."

He hands me two flutes before popping the champagne bottle open and pouring the bubbly liquid.

"What are we celebrating?" I ask.

"Does there have to be a reason?"

"Duh. We're drinking champagne."

"Stick with me, kid. We'll drink champagne whenever you want."

"Your impressions of famous people haven't gotten any better. Good to know."

He lifts his glass toward me. "Let's toast to your new job."

I narrow my eyes on him. "What if I didn't get the job?"

He snorts. "Please. Winter Falls should be begging you to teach their youth."

"They didn't quite beg but Mrs. West did offer me the job."

"I knew it! Congratulations, sweetness." He presses his lips to mine in an all too brief kiss. I whimper as he pulls back.

"Gotta save some for later." He winks before lifting his glass and tapping it against mine.

My eyes widen when I sip the champagne. "This is good."

"Only the best for my Indy."

His gray eyes are full of sincerity, warmth, and love. Hold on. Love? Cash doesn't love me. He doesn't know me. Not anymore.

You still love him, a voice whispers in my head.

Ugh. I wish I could tell my subconscious she's full of rotten bologna. But she's not. I never stopped loving Cash. Never stopped comparing every single man in my life to him. Never stopped yearning to be with him again.

But I'm not going to jump into this relationship with two feet. I'm not seventeen anymore. It was hard enough recovering from Cash abandoning me eleven years ago. If I entwine my life with him and he leaves me again, I'll spend the rest of my life recovering.

It's best to proceed with caution.

I clear my throat. "What else do you have in the basket? I'm starving." My stomach growls as if on cue.

He sets the picnic basket between us and opens it up. "Fried chicken, potato salad, and chocolate chip cookies."

I grab the container of fried chicken and pry it open. "It smells delicious. Tell me you didn't make this." I hold up a drumstick.

He barks out a laugh. "I didn't make the fried chicken."

I raise an eyebrow. It's important to be certain. The one and only time Cash cooked for me, back in the day, he prepared chicken wings. They were burnt to a crisp on the outside and raw on the inside.

He crosses a finger over his heart. "Honest."

I tear a piece of meat off and pop it in my mouth. I groan as the crunchy coating and juicy meat hit my tongue.

"Tease," Cash mutters as he adjusts himself.

"Don't blame me. I'm over here eating my chicken and not bothering you." I'm also a big fat liar who licks her lips and bats her eyelashes.

He growls. "It's not the fried chicken and you know it."

"I don't know. You seemed to walk around with a problem in your pants all the time when we were teenagers."

"Teenager hormones."

I feign a shiver. "The reason I don't teach high school."

"Are you going to tell your mother about your new job?"

I shrug.

He bumps my shoulder. “You need to talk to her.”

I’m not ready to talk to her. I can’t believe she blackmailed Cash into breaking up with me. Doesn’t she want me – her only daughter – to be happy? “We’re not discussing my mother.”

“You need to speak to her at some point.”

I glare at him. “You’re not supposed to be the mature one.”

“Are you saying rockstars can’t be mature? Rockstars can be mature.”

“Old and mature are not the same thing.”

“I’m serious, Indy. You can’t let this fester.”

“Maybe I enjoy letting things fester.”

“I don’t want to drive a wedge between you and your mom.”

I frown at him. “You’re not. This is all on her.”

“She was trying to protect you.”

I snort. “She wasn’t protecting me. She was using you as an instrument to get me to do what she wanted.”

“I don’t understand.”

Dang it! I wasn’t planning on telling him why Mom used the threat she did. I glance away.

He pinches my chin and forces me to face him. “What aren’t you telling me?”

“Who says I’m not telling you something?”

He nods toward my hands. “You’re cracking your knuckles.”

I immediately stop. But it’s too late. Cash knows me too well. Darn him.

“Am I not allowed to have some secrets? Maybe I want to be a woman of mystery?”

He chuckles. "We can play act in the bedroom all you want, but if I'm not allowed to lie to you, you're not allowed to lie to me."

"You're annoying."

"And you're cute when you know I'm right."

"Aren't I always cute?"

He tucks a strand of hair behind my ear and palms my neck. "You're gorgeous and you know it. Now, tell me what has you fidgeting and ready to destroy your knuckles."

"Fine!" I throw my arms in the air. "I told Mom I was deferring my enrollment in college for a year."

His hand spasms. "What were you going to do for a year?"

I roll my eyes. "You know."

He can do what he wants to me. It won't matter. There's no way I'm admitting out loud how I was planning to follow him around like a lovesick puppy after graduation.

"Now it all makes sense," he mutters.

"What makes sense?"

"Your mom never liked me but when she came to talk to me before graduation, she was downright mean. She blamed me for your decision."

I don't want to discuss my mother. I don't want to think about how the woman, who should love me no matter what, doesn't love me at all.

"Can we—"

My question is cut off when Cash's lips crash down on mine.

"Thank you," he mutters against my mouth. He trails kisses along my jaw and down my neck as he draws me into his lap.

"I don't deserve you, Indy, but I'm going to spend the rest of my life working my ass off to make certain you don't regret being with me."

I lace my hands through his hair. "I could never regret you."

Even if I end up with my heart shattered when he leaves Winter Falls, I couldn't regret the time with him.

So much for not jumping in with both feet.

Chapter 23

Family – A whole bunch of people who live to drive you bonkers

Cash

"Are you ready for this?" Indy asks when we stop on the sidewalk in front of the house.

"This is crazy," I say as I stare up at the house. "Why am I going to dinner at my biological father's wife's house?"

"Widow's house," Riley corrects as he and his brothers join us on the sidewalk.

"And you're here because you're family," his twin Brody adds.

Family? Am I really part of their family? I scan the faces of my half-brothers and they each smile at me in greeting. Huh. Maybe I am part of this family.

Indy inches backwards. "I should go."

"Why are you leaving?" Elder asks before she can escape.

She motions toward them. "This appears to be a boys' club."

"Our wives… ahem *my* wife and their girlfriends are inside," Elder says.

Brody rolls his eyes. "He always has to point out how he's married and we're not."

Miller puffs out his chest. "My fiancé and I will get married soon."

Elder snorts. "Really? Has your fiancé agreed on a date yet?"

Miller growls at Elder but Damon steps in between the two. "Can we go inside where it's warm now?"

Brody elbows him. "Someone's California is showing."

"Which is faster – hot or cold?" Elder asks with a grin. "Hot. You can catch a cold."

"You get used to his corny jokes," Riley says as he approaches Indy. "I'm Riley." He captures her hand and kisses her fingers.

I growl and snatch Indy's hand away from him before hauling her close to me.

He grins. "Awesome. I knew you would win her back."

Brody raises an eyebrow. "Really? Last week you bet they wouldn't get back together."

"Reverse psychology."

"Why are you congregating on the sidewalk?" A police officer asks as he strolls toward us.

"Don't worry," Elder says in a whisper-shout. "It's only Peace."

Peace as in the half-brother I haven't met yet? The other brother who was conceived out of wedlock because our biological father apparently couldn't keep it in his pants?

I clear my throat. "Nice to meet you. I'm Cash."

A woman squeals before pushing him out of the way. "I'm Olivia. I'm your biggest fan."

Peace growls before wrapping an arm around her and dragging her to him. "You promised to behave."

"And you believed me? Silly man." She chuckles as she pats his arm.

"You're pregnant. You shouldn't be getting excited."

She rolls her eyes. "You were totally fine with me being excited when you pushed me against the wall five minutes before we left."

Peace groans. "Olivia."

"Peace."

"You're going to be the death of me."

"But oh, what a glorious death it'll be."

"I like her," Indy declares.

Olivia claps. "Awesome. We can be best friends. I have to warn you, though. I have three sisters who think they're the boss of me and one big brother who really thinks he's the boss of all of us."

Indy shrugs. "As long as you agree to add Virginia to our group of friends, I'm in."

Olivia wrests her way out of Peace's hold and grasps Indy's hand before leading her toward the house. "Who's Virginia?"

I start after them. Peace stops me with a hand on my shoulder. "Your girl is perfectly safe."

"She didn't grow up with siblings. I don't want her to be overwhelmed."

Brody barks out a laugh. "Don't worry. She's going to be overwhelmed."

I brush off Peace's hold. "I need to go with her."

"He has my stamp of approval."

I rear back. "Are all of the Bragg brothers crazy?"

"Technically, I'm not a Bragg brother. I'm a Sky. Peace Sky."

He holds out his hand and we shake.

"Nice to meet you," I say because that's what you say when you meet someone and have no idea what else to say.

He chuckles. "Somehow I don't believe you."

"Boys! Are you coming inside or do I need to bring dinner outside?" A woman shouts from the porch.

Damon shivers. "Eat outside in this weather? No thanks."

He marches toward the house with his brothers following him. I trail behind.

When we reach the porch, Peace kisses the woman waiting there before smiling at me. "Cash, meet my mother, Clementine."

"It's lovely to meet you, Mrs. Bragg."

"Oh, I'm not a Bragg. I'm a Sky. Clementine Sky."

My cheeks warm with embarrassment. "I'm sorry. I didn't mean—"

"Don't you worry, young man. We're all family here." She kisses my cheek before herding me inside.

I wait until she bustles into the kitchen before asking Peace, "You brought your mom?"

He chuckles. "As if I could stop her."

I must have misheard. "I'm confused. Your mom is having dinner with the woman…" I trail off as this is getting too awkward for words.

Peace claps me on the back. "My mom is having dinner with the wife of the man she slept with."

"And they get along?"

"Why shouldn't they? Neither one of them did anything wrong." He narrows his eyes on me. "Or do you think my mom is in the wrong?"

I raise my hands and back away. "I don't know what happened. And I never judge."

"Johnny Law," Olivia shouts. "Stop hogging the rockstar."

"Rockstar? Not in this house he isn't," a woman standing in the middle of the room mutters.

"Who is she?" I whisper.

"I'm Daisy Bragg."

A man with long hair clears his throat. "Cox."

She beams at him. "Of course, I'm now Daisy Cox, but I used to be a Bragg."

As in the mother of the Bragg brothers? As in the woman who my mother betrayed by sleeping with her husband? As in the woman my mother vilified because she had what my mother wanted?

I open my mouth to somehow explain my mother wasn't a bad person but the only words to come out are, "I'm sorry."

She pulls me in for a hug. Why is she hugging me? What is happening? I hope I don't appear as awkward as I feel when I pat her back.

She ends the hug but she doesn't release me. She grips my biceps and holds my gaze.

"Don't you dare say you're sorry. It's not your fault my husband cheated on me. It's not your fault your mother had sex with my husband."

I cringe. I know my mother had sex with her husband. I couldn't have been born otherwise. But the idea of my mom and sex? I force those thoughts away. I am not going there.

"But my mother tried to steal your husband."

"Unfortunately, she didn't succeed," she mumbles before her eyes widen. "Oh my gosh. Don't listen to me. Damon Bragg, Sr., was your father and he wasn't a bad man."

"Except for the whole philandering thing," Damon grumbles.

She purses her lips. "You hush or you won't be my favorite anymore."

Damon grins. "Told you I'm the favorite."

A woman slaps him. "Don't be mean to your brothers."

He wraps an arm around her shoulders before kissing her hair. "It's not mean if it's true."

"Are we good?" Mrs. Bragg…er… Cox asks and I return my attention to her.

"I think so. Thank you for being understanding, Mrs. Cox."

"You're family. You call me Daisy."

My heart skips a beat. *Family*. I've always wanted a family. I thought I had one with Indy but I screwed it up. I scan the room to find my girl. She's smiling at me in encouragement. I might have messed it up once, but I'm grabbing hold of my second chance now.

"Thank you, Daisy."

She winks before shoving me in front of her. "Let me introduce you to the rest of the family."

She points to Damon. "You've already met my oldest Damon. The woman with him is his girlfriend Love. They have a daughter Skye who's around here somewhere."

"Hi!" Love waves and smiles in greeting.

"As you know, Elder and Miller are my oldest twins," she says as she motions toward the two men. "Miller is engaged to Eden. She's in the kitchen. You'll meet her soon. And Elder's married to Harmony. Their daughter Robin is having a nap."

"She's the most adorable little girl in the world," Elder declares.

Damon grunts. "I think you mean Skye's the most adorable girl in the world."

"Hey," Brody hollers. "My little one is going to be the best grandchild of them all." He rubs the belly of the woman standing next to him.

Daisy sighs. "You've already met my youngest twins, Riley and Brody. Riley's girlfriend, Moon, is supervising in the kitchen."

"Moon as in Moon's Diner?" I ask.

"She's a chef," Riley answers – the pride clear to hear in his voice.

"And this is Soleil," Brody introduces the pregnant woman he can't keep his hands off of.

I glance around the room at the people gathered. All of whom are somehow related to me. I've gone from being an orphan who had no one to having a huge family.

"I hope you don't expect me to remember everyone's names."

"There'll be a quiz later." Daisy winks up at me. "And we're not done yet." She indicates Clementine.

"I'm Clementine," she says although I already know her name. "This is my husband, Eagle." The man next to her grunts. "I believe you've already met my son, Peace, and his girlfriend, Olivia."

"I'm Indigo," Indy says as she comes to stand next to me. "I'm this guy's girlfriend. I'm also going to steal him away for a minute."

"Go ahead." Daisy motions toward the hallway. "But dinner will be ready in less than ten minutes."

"She means you don't have time to have sex," Olivia explains.

"Thanks for the heads up." I think.

Indy leads me down the hallway to the bathroom. She shuts the door behind her and locks it.

"Are you okay?" Her hazel eyes are full of concern. And love? Dare I hope.

"I don't know. I was just told I can't have sex in ten minutes. I'm feeling challenged." I lift her up on the vanity.

"We are not having sex."

"Boring!" Olivia shouts from the hallway before marching away.

Indy cradles my face. "I'm serious. Are you okay? This is a lot for you."

I lean my forehead against hers. Damn. I love this woman. She gets me. She knows me. In ways no one else ever has. Not even my band members who I consider my family.

"Yeah. I'm okay." I pause before giving her more truths. She deserves all of it. "I was worried before we arrived but everyone has been friendly and Daisy doesn't hate me."

"Of course, she doesn't. You're awesome."

"I do think my brothers are crazy."

"Beyond crazy." She rolls her eyes. "You ready to go back out there?"

"Not yet."

My lips press against hers. This is supposed to be a gentle kiss to show her I appreciate her, I love her, I'm not letting her go. But as soon as her soft lips meet mine and I inhale her strawberry scent and taste her wild candy flavor, I'm a goner.

She moans and I thrust my tongue into her mouth. My fingers dig into her hips as I haul her near.

Bang! Bang!

Indy yanks away from me. Her eyes are wide and her lips are swollen. It's sexy as hell.

"Dinner's ready," Peace calls.

"No fair. You know I wanted to listen to them having sex," Olivia says.

I burst into laughter. "There's never a dull moment around my family."

My family. Those words feel strange. It'll take time before I'm used to them. Used to not being alone.

Now to make Indy part of my family and I'll have everything I've ever needed.

Chapter 24

Teacher – If you're lucky, a famous person who happens to have a free day

Indigo

"Enjoy your lunch," I call to my class of fourth graders as they rush out of the room. "Don't run!"

I don't know why I bother shouting. They're going to run anyway. Luckily for me, their running is not my problem today.

I sigh as I plop down in the chair behind my desk. And I thought six-year-olds were exhausting. Nine-year-olds are worse.

Knock! Knock!

"Come in," I answer. I smile as Cash strolls into my classroom. "What are you doing here?"

He scowls. "Is that how you greet your boyfriend?"

He doesn't give me a chance to answer before leaning over and giving me a hard kiss on the mouth. "Better."

"Easy for you to say. You don't have thirty nine-year-olds who won't hesitate to ask you questions about your boyfriend all afternoon."

I'm whining but it's all for show. I'll stand in front of my class and answer questions about *my boyfriend* until the end of time as long as I can go home to Cash at the end of each day.

The end of each day. I frown. He won't be here every day. As soon as his album is finished, he'll leave Winter Falls.

"What's wrong?"

I force a smile. "Nothing. A bit hungry and ready for lunch is all."

"Lucky for you, I have the perfect remedy." He sets a bag down on my desk.

I sniff. "Did you bring me lunch?"

"How does a hamburger, fries, and a shake sound?"

"Like I'm going to gain fifty pounds." My words don't stop me from digging into the bag and pulling out the food.

"How did you get the diner to give you take-out food?" I ask around a bite of my burger.

Take-out food isn't normally done in Winter Falls since the packaging is bad for the environment and everything bad for the environment is banned in town. It's weird, but I'll get used to it. Eventually.

He settles on the desk before opening his own burger. "As it happens, the diner is owned by my sister-in-law, Moon. I'm her favorite brother-in-law."

I snort. "What did you promise her?"

"Signed t-shirts from all the band members. She's going to display them on the walls of the diner."

"Aren't you worried your fans will find out and chase you down?"

"Not really. Our PA, Aurora, monitors social media to check where the fans think we're hiding."

"They think you're hiding?"

He sighs. "If we're not seen out partying every night, we're hiding. If we are out every night, we're out of control."

"Sounds annoying."

"It is what it is. Aurora posts pictures of us in different places to keep the fans guessing where we are."

"Do you worry they'll find you?"

"Nah. The fans are the reason we can do what we love." He presses his thigh against mine. "But I'm not here to discuss my fans. How is your first day going?"

I can't help the smile from spreading across my face. "Good. Tiring but good."

"I bet you're an awesome teacher. All the boys probably have crushes on you."

I roll my eyes. "They're nine. They don't have crushes."

"You'd be surprised. When I was nine…"

I hold up a hand. "I do not want to know about your crush on Mrs. What's Her Name."

"No? Mrs. What's Her Name is now Ms. What's Her Name and showed up at one of my concerts."

My mouth drops open. "You're kidding."

"Nope. Turns out I was her favorite student ever."

I snort. "Oh please. You were a horrible student. She just chased you because you're hot."

"You think I'm hot?"

I slap his thigh. "We're in a school."

He waggles his eyebrows. "Being in a school never stopped you before from telling me how hot I am. Or was it how hot you were for me?"

"You're a menace."

He grins. "And proud of it."

"Be careful before Mrs. West bans you from entering the high school."

"Mrs. West would never ban anyone from the building for discussing sex," the teacher from across the hall says as he enters my classroom.

"Really?" Cash raises an eyebrow. "Tell me more."

"The principal is on a mission to teach the world about safe sex. She keeps a jar of condoms on her desk. They're flavored."

Cash barks out a laugh. "Winter Falls is growing on me."

The teacher steps forward and holds out his hand. "Bob O'Neill."

"Cash Evans."

"Um…" He glances behind him where several teachers are peeking into my classroom. "I've been elected the spokesperson."

I stand in front of Cash to block him from their view. "Not on my watch."

Cash presses against my back. "It's okay, Indy."

"No, it's not. They can't take advantage of you because you're famous. It's not okay."

Bob wrings his hands. "To be fair, we don't want to take advantage of him because he's famous."

I cross my arms over my chest and stare him down.

"We want to take advantage of him because he's a professional musician."

I snort. "Well, then, okay."

"It's not a problem, Indy. What can I help you with?" he asks Bob and the group since the other teachers have now invaded my room.

Bob clears his throat. "Is there any chance you'd teach some kids a few tricks on how to play the guitar?"

A man pushes to the front of the group. "I teach high school band but my guitar skills aren't the best. I'm more of a keyboard player."

Cash steps forward but I block him. "You don't have to do this."

He shrugs. "I'm not doing anything else this afternoon."

"Aren't you supposed to be recording an album?"

"Jett's AWOL and Gibson has a hangover."

"Jett's AWOL? Do we need to organize a search team to find him? The nature around Winter Falls is not a joke. He could be lost or bit by an animal or—"

He places a finger on my lips. "Jett's fine. He's not out in the woods. He's probably still passed out in whoever's bed he landed in last night."

"Did you at least try to call him?"

He kisses my forehead. "Stop. You don't need to worry about him."

I give in on a huff.

Cash grins at the high school band teacher. "Okay, Mr.... I'm sorry. I didn't get your name."

"It's Jupiter," he says as they shake hands.

"Jupiter?"

"I'm a Winter Falls native."

Cash rubs his hands together. "Do you have a class of kids or just a few who need help?"

I nearly try to stop Cash again but I notice the sparkle in his eyes. He's excited to help these kids.

"I'm not the best guitar player. Dylan plays lead guitar for *Cash & the Sinners*, but I do all right."

Their discussion quickly delves into technical music stuff I don't understand. I probably should let them go, but I notice the group of teachers following them and join in.

A female teacher I have yet to meet bumps my shoulder. "I can't believe you're dating Cash from *Cash & the Sinners*."

"What's he like?" another woman asks.

"Does he sing to you in bed?"

"How about those fingers of his? Does he strum you like a guitar?"

"Has he asked you to do a threesome?"

"I'm up for a threesome."

"Your husband would kill you."

"Nope. Cash is on my list."

I hold up my hands. "Ladies. Ladies. Ladies."

Several eager eyes focus on me. "I've known Cash since he was a teenager who wore dirty jeans with holes in them. He's not some famous dude to me. He's Cash."

"You love him?"

I roll my eyes. I'm not telling these strangers I love Cash when I haven't managed to tell Cash yet. Or again.

"Do you want to watch Cash teach a bunch of snot-nosed teenagers how to play the guitar or do you want to grill me? Spoiler alert. I won't be revealing anything sexual about Cash."

"Bummer," Mrs. West says as she joins us. "I was hoping for some tips for the bedroom."

My mouth drops open.

"Don't look so shocked. Middle-aged mothers have sex, too."

Before I can answer, a cheer goes up in the music room as Cash saunters in. I am not missing out on watching him teach. Whenever he's near a guitar, his body lights up with excitement. He was always meant to be a musician.

I enter the room in time to watch Cash raise a hand. Everyone immediately quiets. The man has stage presence in a classroom.

"I'm Cash and I'm apparently your teacher for the next hour."

Pride fills my chest as I watch him show the students a few chords on the guitar. He's patient and gentle with them. He would make a great teacher.

He glances up at me and winks.

My heart bursts with love for him as the truth finally sinks in. He didn't leave me to become a rockstar. He's told me time and time again he didn't leave to become famous, but I didn't believe him. Not until now. He left me because my mom wanted to control my life and everyone in it.

I'm going to have to deal with my mother and her betrayal someday, because what she did is not okay. All this time I've bent over backwards to try and gain her approval. I'm beginning to realize she'll never approve of me. Never love me unconditionally the way a mother should.

But those problems are for another day. For now, I'll enjoy watching Cash teach some high schoolers how to play the guitar. I couldn't be prouder of the man he's become.

Chapter 25

Crash and burn – What happens whenever Dylan is near Virginia

Cash

"You ready?" I ask Indy as I open the door for her and escort her outside.

She grins up at me. "Winter Falls' festivals are the best."

I shut the door behind us before grasping her hand, and we begin walking toward Main Street.

"I hope you're okay with the band joining us," I mutter when I notice my bandmates coming our way on the sidewalk.

"Of course, it's okay. They're your friends."

"What a weird way to say pain in the ass."

She elbows me. "Be nice."

"Hey, Indigo," Dylan greets her with a kiss and I growl at him. He chuckles. "You're too easy."

I wrap an arm around Indy and pull her near. "Get your own girl."

"Nah. We travel around too much."

The happiness bleeds from Indy's face at Dylan's reminder of how our lives are not of the typical 'nine-to-five and home every night' variety. I glare at him, but he shrugs. Asshole. I'll get him back.

"What are we doing today anyway?" Jett asks.

"It's Eostare," Indy says.

"Do you mean Easter?" Gibson asks.

She giggles. "This is Winter Falls. They wouldn't have a festival for anything as normal as Easter."

"I'll bite. What's Eostare?" Jett asks.

"According to my students who were appalled I didn't know the legend, Eostre is the fertility goddess of humans and crops. She mated with the solar god of the spring, Equinox, and nine months later gave birth to a god child."

Jett perks up. "I want to be the solar god of the spring."

"I don't think you choose to be a god. I think you're chosen," Indy says.

"We'll see," he sings as we continue toward Main Street where the festival is happening.

We round the corner and skid to a halt. "What the hell?"

Downtown is completely packed. There are people everywhere. On the road, on the sidewalks, in the shops. There's no space to move between them.

"This reminds me of a rock festival," Fender grumbles.

"Except we don't have backstage passes," Dylan adds.

"We can go back to the house," Indy suggests, "if you guys are uncomfortable."

I scowl. "We're not a bunch of pansies."

Dylan chuckles. "Says the man who dove into a patch of pansies."

I glare at him. "You would have done the same thing."

Gibson puffs out his chest. "Not me. I don't flee when the ladies are begging for my attention."

Fender grunts. "Man whore."

Gibson wags his finger at him. "They don't pay me, thus I'm not a whore."

Jett snorts. "And still, he can't get as many women as me."

Indy tugs on my hand. "Is this what you guys do when you're touring around? Compare how many women you've slept with?"

"Except for Cash," Gibson butts in. "He's practically a born again virgin."

I slash my hand over my throat in an effort to get him to shut up. It doesn't work. It never does. I don't know why I bother to try at this point.

"The pansy field was not the first time he ran from female admirers," Dylan adds. "Remember the time he claimed to have diarrhea to get a fan to leave him alone."

"As I recall, it didn't work. She followed him into the bathroom." Jett chuckles.

"With an entire pharmacy to help him," Gibson continues. "But without any clothes."

I glare at them. "And you assholes didn't stop her."

Dylan snorts. "Why would we stop her?"

Fuck. Indy's going to freak with all these stories of me and other women. But when I start to explain, I realize she's not paying attention. She's waving Virginia over to our group. They hug in greeting.

Dylan smiles at her. "Hi, Virginia."

She scowls. "Hello, Dylan."

"When are you going to put me out of my misery and go out on a date with me?"

Her scowl deepens. "Why would I go out with you? You don't even know who I am."

He wiggles his eyebrows. "Thus, a date to get to know you."

"You're an idiot," she mumbles before facing Indy again. "I'm going to the craft fair. Let's plan to meet up for coffee soon."

She doesn't wait for Indy's agreement before marching off.

"Burn!" Gibson yells.

Jett doubles over laughing. "I wish I had recorded the entire interaction. Social media would go wild watching Dylan get rejected."

Dylan's nostrils flare. "You're not putting my private life on social media."

"Duh. I didn't record it."

I lean close to whisper in Indy's ear. "Are you going to tell Dylan we went to high school with Virginia?"

"And ruin my live soap opera? No way."

I kiss her hair. "Thank you."

"For what?"

For giving me the perfect way to get back at Dylan for being an asshole.

"For being you."

She narrows her eyes at me but before she can question me someone shrieks. "CASH!"

I duck my head while the rest of the band forms a circle around us to shield me and Indy from any onlookers.

"I saw Cash from *Cash & the Sinners.* He's here!"

"Let's go," Fender orders as he herds us away from the crowd.

"Don't let them get away."

Shit. We're in trouble here and we don't have any security. I don't care about myself but I don't want Indy hurt. These situations can get dicey as we learned one late night in Boise, Idaho of all places. I never thought I'd be glad Jett used to drag race growing up.

"Stop right there, young lady."

"Get out of my way, old hag."

"What's going on?" I ask since I can't see anything besides my bandmates.

"I caution you against calling the police dispatcher an old hag."

I recognize the voice. "Is that Peace?" I ask although no one in the band would recognize my half-brother since they haven't met my family yet.

"Is Peace a cop?" Jett asks. I nod. "It's probably him. And he's not alone."

"The force is out in full," Gibson adds.

Our circle loosens once we realize the police are on the scene. We form a line and smile and wave at the fans.

Indy steps away from me but I snatch her hand to keep her close. She's not going anywhere. Not now. Not ever. I don't care if my no longer being single causes a shit storm on social media and Aurora tries to skin me alive. Indy's mine.

The gossip gals march to the front of the group.

"Good thing I brought the megaphone," Sage says.

"Why did you bring a megaphone to a festival?" Feather asks.

"The same reason I brought the binoculars. You never know when it'll come in handy." Cayenne lifts a pair of binoculars.

Dylan grins. "The gossip gals are awesome."

I don't disagree.

"May I have your attention, please?" Sage blares through the megaphone.

"You have a choice to make," she continues. "You can turn in your telephones and cameras or you can leave Winter Falls. What you won't do is snap pictures of the band and post them on the Insta."

"Oh yeah? Who's going to stop us?"

Peace and the rest of the police force form a line in front of us. I'm afraid the three men won't be enough to hold back the fans. Don't get me wrong. I love our fans. Without them, we wouldn't be able to do what we love to do – play music – but this situation is not under control.

Before I can order the band to make a run for it, my other half-brothers join the line. They cross their arms over their chests and glare at the crowd.

"We'll stop you," Miller grumbles.

"No one is attacking my brother," Damon declares.

"Even if he isn't a twin." Riley glances over his shoulder and winks at me.

At their words, a hole I didn't realize existed in my chest begins to fill. My brothers – my *brothers* – don't hate me for being a bastard their dad created when he stepped out on their mom. They care about *me.*

They told me as much before, but I didn't believe them. Not until this moment when they're protecting me. I've never had a sibling to protect me before.

"Brother?" Jett asks.

"Surprise! I found my dad." I motion to the line of my brothers. "And my family."

"About time you realized we're your family," Elder says.

"You're part of the Bragg Brother Bunch now," Brody adds.

Hell yeah, I am. And damn proud of it, too.

"No wonder Dylan was talking about your family," Gibson mutters.

Peace places a metal box on the ground and people line up to throw their phones in it. Within minutes, the crowd has dispersed and hardly anyone is paying attention to us. My brothers salute me before heading off.

"See you at the next family dinner," Damon calls.

"The story of how you found your family will have to wait. I have business to attend to." Gibson nods toward the group of women across the street who keep peeking at us from beneath their eyelashes before marching toward them.

Jett chases after him. "Don't forget me."

Fender sighs before following them.

"You good?" Dylan asks. At my nod, he grins. "Excellent. I have a librarian to find."

"I guess it's just you and me." I smile down at Indy but she's frowning.

"What's wrong? I swear this isn't a normal occurrence. You don't have to worry about your safety when you're with me. I will always protect you."

She blows out a breath. "I'm not afraid," she claims but she won't look at me.

I pinch her chin and force her to meet my gaze. "Then, what is it?"

She stays quiet for a long time until I'm convinced she isn't going to answer. "We need to talk."

Everything in me screams *NO!* We are not having any kind of discussion that begins with her saying the words 'the talk'. She is not dumping me. Not after I've finally won her back and we've begun again.

I inhale a deep breath and force myself to calm down before I end up yelling. Yelling won't do me any good.

"Let's find somewhere private."

I'll let her have her say and then I'll convince her she's wrong.

Chapter 26

Bullshit – Excuses you come up with to hide how scared you are

INDIGO

Cash scans the area and frowns.

"It's busy everywhere. Let's go home."

Let's go home. Oh, how I wish those words were true. That we were walking toward *our home.* A home with Cash is all I've ever wanted. Not Cash the rockstar. Cash the boy I fell in love with.

We turn around and start toward the house. Before we can cross the street, a squirrel darts out in front of me.

I grasp my chest. "I didn't…"

I trail off when Katy Purry rushes out of the bushes after the squirrel.

"Get back here!" a man shouts as he follows after them.

I chase after him. "Don't you dare hurt, Katy Purry!"

He stops and whirls around to confront me and I nearly bump into him.

He glares at me. "I wouldn't hurt an animal. Who do you think I am?"

I don't know. I have no idea who this man is. I've never seen him before.

I hold out my hand. "I'm Indigo."

"No time for niceties. I have a chipmunk to save."

"Too bad he wasn't on his leash," Cash says.

"Leash? What are you talking about?" I ask.

"This is Forest," Cash points to the man. "He enjoys walking his chipmunks on a leash. At least he's wearing pants today."

Wearing pants today? Why wouldn't he wear pants?

"I don't keep Dale on his leash in my backyard." Forest scowls at me. "But I didn't expect a cat to show up either."

I cringe. "Katy Purry won't hurt your chipmunk." I hope. I'm afraid my kitty isn't an innocent as I proclaim she is.

"And she didn't kill a bird yesterday either," Cash mutters beside me and I elbow him. He's not helping things.

The bushes next to us rustle before my kitty prances out. "See?" I point. "She didn't harm anyone."

"Where's Dale?" Forest falls to his knees to search the bushes.

"Grab the devil cat," Cash orders. "I'll help search for the chipmunk."

"My cat is not the devil," I mumble before approaching Katy Purry. "Here, kitty. Here, kitty."

My cat stops and sits. She begins licking her paws as she watches me.

"There's a good kitty," I say as I reach for her.

I swear she scoffs as if she can understand what I'm saying and disagrees with me. Is there such a thing as a cat whisperer? Maybe I should contact one since my kitty and Cash don't get along.

Whoa. I'm getting way ahead of myself.

Cash never said he was sticking around. He's staying until the band finishes their latest album. Which won't take a year no matter what he says. The fans have been clamoring for another concert tour already. Soon enough he'll be gone and where does that leave me? Leave us?

Knock it off, Indy. Standing on the sidewalk while my cat eyeballs me is not the moment for deep contemplation about my romantic relationship.

"Come on, Katy. Let's go home." I bend to pick her up but she swipes at me before rushing off.

"I got him," Forest shouts before emerging from the bushes with a chipmunk cradled in his arms. "Let's go home and get you a treat. You've had a traumatic morning," he murmurs to the animal as he walks away.

"Cash?" I call. "You can come out now."

He crawls out of the bushes and stands. I pull a twig out of his hair.

He scowls. "If you tell anyone about me crawling around in the bushes…"

"You'll what?"

He wraps an arm around my waist and tugs me to him. "I'll spank your sweet cheeks."

Heat rushes through me straight to my core at his words. I've never been spanked before but the idea of Cash spanking my naked bottom sounds intriguing.

"No spanking," I claim but my words come out breathy.

He winks. "You'll change your mind."

He stares at my lips and I bite my bottom one. He groans before releasing me.

"You wanted to talk."

His reminder douses my arousal better than a bucket of ice water. I nod and we walk back to the house in silence.

"Do you want a beer?" I ask when we enter.

"I'm good."

Dang. So much for my stalling.

I sit on the couch. I expect Cash to sit next to me, but he doesn't. He perches on the coffee table between my legs.

I open my mouth to tell him to give me some space but he holds up a hand to stop me. "No. I'll have the 'talk' with you but I will be touching you the entire time."

"Why didn't you stay and say hi to your fans?" I blurt out before I can stop myself.

His brow wrinkles. "I waved to them and said hi."

I roll my eyes. "But you didn't greet them the way Gibson and Jett did."

He scowls. "Do not compare me to those man whores."

He's right. I'm being unfair.

"Maybe you don't sleep with all of your groupies, but—"

"I don't sleep with any of the groupies," he interrupts to say.

I do not want to think about him having sex with other women. Moving on. "But you are on the road all the time."

"I'm in a band. We tour. But we're not on the road all the time."

"Semantics. You're never home."

"Maybe because I never had a home before."

"And now you're ready for a home?" If I sound skeptical, it's because I am.

He sighs. "You don't get it, do you?"

"Get what?"

"You, Indigo Scott, are my home. Wherever you are, is where I want to be."

I frown. "Be realistic. You can't always be where I am."

"I know. The kids at the school would find it mighty weird if I sat in the back of the class the whole day."

I slap his thigh. "Stop making light of my concerns."

He clears his throat. "I'm not trying to make light of your concerns. I'm trying to show you they're not important."

I scowl. "What I think isn't important?"

"Of course, it's important. And I will sit right here until my ass falls asleep listening to you, but you're not hearing what I'm saying."

"What are you saying?"

"I'm saying I want to make a home with you whether it's here in Winter Falls or back in San Diego or in Timbuktu."

"Mali isn't exactly a safe place to live now."

"Scratch Timbuktu." He cradles my face in his hands. "Why are you scared?"

"I'm not scared." I'm terrified. He wants to build a home with me? He's a famous rockstar, I'm an elementary school teacher.

"Stop."

I widen my eyes. "Stop what?"

"Stop trying to come up with an excuse to pull away from me."

I blow out a breath. "It's not excuses if they're true."

"Okay. Hit me."

"Hit you?"

"With whatever bullshit you've come up with to convince yourself it won't work between us."

"It's not bullshit. I was there. Your fans nearly caused a riot in Winter Falls."

"And?"

"And you're a famous rockstar. You dumped me to become a rockstar."

His nostrils flare. "I did not dump you to become a rockstar. I thought we cleared this up already."

I flinch. No, he didn't dump me to become a rockstar. My *mother* is the reason he dumped me. But I don't want to think about how the woman who birthed me doesn't love me. Ignoring those problems for now.

"Okay. Fine. You didn't dump me to become a rockstar."

"But..."

"But you are one. Women chase you everywhere."

"So?"

How can he not understand what I'm saying?

"They're not you, Indy. You're the one I want."

"But I'm here in Winter Falls and you're wherever."

"Then, I'll move to Winter Falls." He shrugs as if it's no big deal.

"You can't snap your fingers and – boom! – your home is now in Winter Falls."

"You're right. Let me alert Aurora. She'll handle everything." He digs in his pocket for his phone.

"You're serious?"

"As a broken guitar string."

"What if I leave Winter Falls after the year is up and sell Grandma's house?"

"Then, I'll call Aurora and she'll handle moving us back to San Diego."

"I need to meet this Aurora."

"Don't be jealous. She's not interested in me."

"I'm not jealous." I'm totally jealous. This Aurora seems to know everything about Cash and his life. I don't know anything. Maybe I should have read all those magazines with his stupidly handsome face on the cover.

"Are we done?"

"Done?"

"Have I convinced you I'm serious about this relationship?"

I try to come up with another reason to push him away but the annoying man has an answer for every issue I bring up. Am I still worried about him being gone all the time? Yes. But if I want to give this relationship a try, I need to give him a chance to prove he's worth my time. No matter how much it scares me.

"For now."

"Good." He stands and throws me over his shoulder.

"What are you doing?" I squeal.

"Showing you I'm worth the risk."

His hand kneads my butt. It feels good but my clothes are in the way. I want to feel his hand touching my naked skin. And not just his hand. His mouth, too. Definitely his mouth. My body tingles in anticipation.

"I might need a lot of convincing."

"We've got all the time in the world, sweetness. All the time in the world."

Chapter 27

Trust – Not easy to earn, but super easy to lose

CASH

In my hurry, I trip on the stairs and nearly drop Indy.

"Oh my god!" Her fists pound on my back. "Put me down before you drop me and you can't put me back together again."

I tighten my hold on her legs. "I'm not dropping you and you aren't Humpty Dumpty."

"I can still fall and break."

I carry her to her bedroom and lay her on the bed before covering her with my body. "I will always protect you. You are not getting hurt on my watch."

Her eyes warm with love. Love? Does she still love me? Or love me again? Damn, I hope so. Because I love her more than life itself. I will give her anything. She thinks moving to Winter Falls is a big deal. She has no idea the lengths I'll go to, to give her what she wants.

I brush the hair off her forehead. "You're my Indy. My everything."

I stop myself before declaring my undying love. Words are just words. Easily spoken. I'll show her how I feel.

I meld my lips to hers. She immediately opens up to me on a sigh. I dive in. Anxious to sample her strawberry and cream taste. The flavor fills my mouth and lungs. It's intoxicating.

Indy clutches my shoulders and her fingers dig into my skin through my sweater. I'm going to have bruises in the morning, and I don't care. She can give me all the bruises she wants.

I press my hard length against her core and her legs fall open. I fit my hips into the gap and thrust my cock against her. She begins rubbing herself up and down me causing all the blood in my body to rush to my cock.

I grasp her hips to slow her movements before things get messy. Although, if memory serves me correctly, Indy never complained when I came in my jeans before, but we're no longer teenagers. I'm a man and it's my mission to show her how I feel. Not get off while we're both still dressed.

Indy wrenches her lips from mine. "Why are you stopping me?" She pouts.

"Because I have plans."

Her hazel eyes flare until the blue overcomes the green and brown. Those hazel eyes of hers have always captivated me. What color will they turn when she comes? I can't wait to find out.

"Are you going to execute these supposed plans or stare at me all day long?"

"I could stare at you all day," I tease.

"Really?" She wiggles underneath me and I groan at the friction against my cock.

"You're cruel."

"You're the one who slowed things down. Not me."

"Because the first time you come won't be when you're dressed."

"It won't?" She raises her eyebrows. "When will it be? I'm on a schedule here."

I call her bluff. "Do you have somewhere else to be?"

"Maybe I want to go back to the Eostare festival and win the egg hunt."

"The egg hunt?" What is she talking about? Obviously, I'm not doing this right if she can form coherent sentences.

"Hands above your head," I order. She shivers. She'll deny it until her dying day but she loves when I order her around.

Her eyes meet mine as she slowly raises her hands.

"Grab the headboard," I growl.

"You better make it worth my while." The sassiness of her words is ruined by how excited she sounds.

I nip her bottom lip. "Have I ever not made it worth your while?"

She pretends to consider the question. "No?"

"I'll ask again after your second orgasm."

"Second? Slowing down in your old age."

I don't remind her we're the same age. I'm done talking. I grasp the waistband of her leggings and yank them down her legs together with her underwear.

I glance down at Indy lying on the bed. Her legs are short but curvy. Her hips flare out, inviting me to lay between them. She's my dream.

Except she's still half-dressed. I gather the fabric of her sweater from around her waist and draw it up and over her head. I consider using the material to tie her hands to the headboard but now is not the time for playing. Now is the time to make love to Indy. To show her how I feel.

I throw the sweater over my shoulder.

"This is handy," I mumble as I play with the front fastening of her bra. I trail my finger along the lacy edge.

"Take it off."

"In time," I say to tease her.

"You're cruel."

I lean over and fit my mouth around her nipple before sucking. Her back arches off the bed.

"Was that cruel?"

I don't give her a chance to answer before yanking her bra cups down to expose her perky breasts. "What about this? Is this cruel?"

I pinch her nipple and she moans.

"Or what about this?" I ask before teasing her nipple with my teeth.

She thrashes on the bed as I give up all pretense of teasing her. I massage and knead her breasts as I suck on them.

Her legs lock around my hips and she grinds her core against my cock hidden behind my jeans. Why am I wearing jeans? I'm supposed to be making love to this woman. Not having a quick fuck with my clothes on. She's not some groupie.

I release her nipple with a pop and roll off the bed.

"Where are you going?"

I answer by ripping my sweater off. She licks her lips as her gaze rakes over my chest. All those boring hours spent lifting weights were worth it for the look in her eyes. I snap my jeans open and draw the zipper down. My cock pops out. Pointing straight to Indy. He knows what he wants.

I tug on it a few times and she sits up before reaching for me. I wag my finger at her. "Did I say you could move?"

She flops back on the bed. "You didn't say I couldn't move."

I chuckle as I shove my jeans down my legs. Once I'm completely naked, I crawl back into bed with her.

I position myself in between her hips. She widens her legs to make room for me and I hitch my cock at her entrance.

I'm not even inside her yet and I can feel how hot and wet she is for me. I inhale a deep breath to get myself under control before I thrust into her. *Making love. Making love.* I chant the words over and over in my head.

I push inside. Heaven. She feels like heaven. I glance down at our joining and swear.

"What's wrong?"

I grit my teeth. "I forgot a condom." I try to force myself to retreat but my cock is running the show and he's not going anywhere.

"No need."

"No need?" Is she saying what I think she's saying?

"I get the shot. We're covered."

My cock is fully on board but I need to make sure. "The shot is only good to prevent pregnancy."

She ducks her chin but not before I notice her cheeks flame. "I haven't been with anyone for over a year."

"Except me," I remind her.

She rolls her eyes. "Except you."

I blow out a breath and admit the truth. "I haven't been with anyone in a year either."

Her brow furrows. "Are you serious?" I nod. "But what about—"

My growl cuts her off. "Do not mention fans or groupies while we are in bed together."

"You're not lying?"

"I'm not lying." I wouldn't lie about anything as important as this. In fact, I won't lie to Indy at all anymore. I kept the truth about what her mother said to me hidden and what good did it do?

She studies my face and I let her see everything. The truth, my love for her, my regret about leaving her – everything.

"I trust you."

Warmth spreads throughout my body. Indy trusts me. Maybe convincing her to fall in love with me again won't be as difficult as I thought.

"And I trust you."

"Naturally. I'm perfect." She winks.

"You're sure?" I ask one more time. I don't want her to consider me a mistake.

She wraps her legs around my waist and lifts her hips. "I'm more than sure."

I sink into her until my balls slap her skin. Fuck. Fuck. Fuck. I can feel everything without a condom between us. I've never had sex without a condom before. Not even when Indy and I were kids did we forego condoms.

Think of baseball scores. I hate baseball. The lyrics to your new song. Anything! I can't come now. Not on the first thrust.

Indy tightens her inner muscles around me as she arches her back and rubs her breasts against my naked chest. Oh shit. I begin to recite the alphabet backwards. What comes after w?

"Move, Cash."

I withdraw at a snail's pace enjoying the feel of every inch of her before plunging into her again. I start up a slow but steady pace. Indy meets each thrust and we settle into a leisurely tempo.

"Sex… with you… is… awesome," she gasps out.

"This isn't sex. This is making love."

Her eyes pop open at my words. "I'm almost there."

"Are you ready to come for me, Indy?" She nods. "Then, come, sweetness. Come all over my cock. Let me feel you."

Her legs tremble and her eyes begin to shut.

"No. Keep your eyes open."

She drags them open and our gazes lock as her mouth falls open and she moans.

"Yeeees."

Her walls strangle my cock and it's all I can do to keep the pace steady to draw out her climax. When she collapses against the bed, I increase my thrusts until I'm pounding into her. Her breasts jiggle and I'm done.

"Indy!" I shout as I come.

I collapse on top of her. I should roll off her. I'm probably squishing her. But I can't move.

"I love you, Indigo."

I wait for a response. When none comes, I glance down at her. She's out cold.

I chuckle as I roll off of the bed and go in search of a washcloth to clean her up.

Chapter 28

The L-word – Four letters that are incredibly hard to say

INDIGO

I sigh as I wake. Muscles I forgot I had are sore from spending the day in bed with Cash yesterday. I stretch my arms above my head before reaching for Cash. I pat the bed but he's not there.

"Cash?"

When he doesn't answer, I scan the room for a note. Maybe he went to the studio to do some recording. But I don't see one. Panic begins to claw at me but I push it down. Cash didn't leave me. He lives here. For now.

"Indy! Get down here and do something about your cat before I decide to try cat meat for breakfast."

"On my way!"

I jump out of bed and throw a robe over my naked body before hurrying down the stairs.

"Don't you dare…"

My words trail off at the scene before me. Cash is at the stove. He's shirtless and his jeans are slung low over his hips. Oh my. His back muscles bunch as he moves the spatula around the pan.

"You learned to cook?"

"Judging from the burnt toast, no, I haven't," he mutters before glancing over his shoulder and smiling at me.

I want to see that smile on his face every single morning for the rest of my life. I want him in my bed every night for the rest of my life. I plain want him. I always have and I always will.

"I love you." The words are out before I can stop them. I slam a hand on my mouth but there's no way I can shove those words back inside.

Cash throws the spatula down and stalks toward me. He uncurls my fingers from my face.

"You love me?"

I shake my head.

"Are you lying?"

I shrug.

He smiles. "You're definitely lying."

I glare at him.

"You're adorable when you're mad."

"I am not adorable. I'm not a two-year-old."

"I think I proved you're an adult last night." He waggles his eyebrows. "Several times."

I roll my eyes. Leave it to a man to make every conversation about sex.

He frames my face with his hands and meets my gaze. "In case there's any confusion, I love you, Indigo." I gasp but he doesn't stop. "I loved you when we were teenagers and I could barely figure out how to put a condom on, let alone how to please you. I loved you for the decade we were apart. And I love you now more than ever. I will always love you."

"You weren't a horrible lover when we were teenagers," I say since I'm too busy reeling from the amount of times he said the word 'love' to make any sense.

He chuckles before pressing his lips to mine. I dig my hands into his shoulders and pull him near as I open for him. He thrusts his tongue into my mouth. When his taste of coffee and musk and something just Cash hits me, I moan.

He angles my head to dive in deeper. Fine by me. Being kissed by Cash is unlike being kissed by any other man. When he kisses me, his full concentration is on me. Not his phone. Not the clock. Me.

Beep! Beep! Beep!

He yanks away before rushing to the stove. "Shit. I forgot about the eggs."

While he shoves the pan under the water, I wave a towel in front of the smoke alarm until it stops beeping.

"I think I ruined breakfast."

"Ya think?"

He lifts the pan to show me the burnt eggs.

I giggle. "Burnt eggs to go with the burnt toast."

"I'll ask Aurora to buy some new pans and put them in my stuff when she ships it."

I try to stop myself from scowling but it doesn't work.

"What's wrong?" Cash drops the pan in the sink and stalks toward me until my back hits the counter. He places his hands on each side of me to cage me in. "What's wrong, Indy?"

"Nothing."

"You always look like you swallowed a lemon?"

"You just tried to start Grandma's house on fire. I'm allowed to be annoyed with you right now."

He leans close to whisper in my ear. "You weren't annoyed when I had my tongue down your throat."

I cross my arms over my chest to hide my shiver. "That was before the fire."

"There was no fire. There was barely any smoke. And you weren't annoyed until..." He swears underneath his breath before cradling my face in his hands. "There's no reason to be jealous."

"I'm not jealous. Why would I be jealous? Who do I have to be jealous of?"

"Aurora's the band's personal assistant. Our relationship is strictly professional."

I play with the hairs on his chest to avoid looking into his eyes as I confess, "But she knows you."

"Knowing what size jeans I wear doesn't equal knowing me. The real me. The only people who know the real me are Dylan, Fender, Gibson, Jett, and you."

"Really?"

"Besides, Aurora's hung up on someone else."

"Who?"

"If I tell you, I'll have to kill you."

I try to laugh but I can't. "But I missed all these years with you. We're not the same people we were back in high school."

He takes my hand and places it over his heart. "In here, I'm the same. I'm the same boy you fell in love with when I stuck up for you in front of those cheerleaders."

"Witches."

He smiles. "I wish I could erase the past decade. I wish I had never allowed your mother to convince me to end our relationship. But I can't. And I'm not wasting my wishes on the past."

"What's with the wishes? Do you have a genie in a bottle hidden somewhere?"

He presses his hips against me. "No, but I have something hidden in my jeans. You want to explore?"

"Could you seriously be any cornier?"

"I think you mean hornier."

"How can you be horny? We had sex all day long yesterday."

"No, we didn't."

I scratch my chin. "We didn't? Who was inside me most of yesterday if it wasn't you?"

He growls. "Only I will be inside you from here on out."

"Yes, sir. Whatever you say, sir."

His eyes flare. "I love it when you follow my orders."

"Too bad I don't enjoy following orders."

He nips my earlobe. "You more than enjoy following orders. You just don't want to enjoy following orders."

I have no response since he's right, so I tilt my head to offer him my neck instead. He bites and nibbles his way along my jaw until he reaches my lips.

"You have perfect bowtie lips," he murmurs as he licks them.

I press against him ready to continue our kiss from before but he leans back away from me. "Are we good?"

"Not yet but I assume we'll be feeling good pretty soon."

"You will. I guarantee it."

"Is this a money-back guarantee?"

He tweaks my nose. "Stop being a smart alec for five seconds. I'm trying to check if you're okay with the whole Aurora situation."

I blow out a breath as I contemplate my answer. I don't want to admit I'm jealous although it's pretty obvious I am. But it's more than mere jealousy.

"I'm sad we lost ten years together because my mom's a bitch." I hate to swear but witch isn't a strong enough word to describe my mother.

"Hey now. Don't call your mom a bitch."

"What if it's true?" What if my mom doesn't love me? Will I ever stop yearning for her love?

"This is why I didn't want to explain why I left you on the day of our high school graduation. I didn't want to drive a wedge between you and your mom."

I scowl. "I think she drove the wedge herself when she refused to show up for Grandma's funeral."

"I'm sorry she wasn't there."

"It's probably better she wasn't." I sigh. "She never would have honored Grandma's wishes."

"You need to call her."

I do, but I'm not ready. Not when there's a possibility our relationship will be forever ruined after I confront her about what she did to Cash.

"Stop being reasonable. Where's my rockstar Cash?"

"I can be reasonable and be a rockstar."

"As long as Aurora folds your panties for you."

"You're in trouble now." He tickles my ribs. I try batting him away but he doesn't let up until he picks me up and throws me over his shoulder.

"Don't drop me."

He pretends to stumble. "I'll try not to."

I slap his back. "There is no try. Only do."

"I love you, my Star Wars geek."

"Knowing one quote from Yoda doesn't make me a Star Wars geek."

He throws me on the bed. "Are you done stalling yet?"

"Stalling?"

He drops on top of me. "Tell me you love me, Indigo."

I sigh. He's right. I have been stalling. Which is silly. He already knows I love him. And I told him as much, too. But it was an accident. Saying the words on purpose feels big. I'm not ready to say them.

I glance up at Cash and our gazes meet. His eyes are full of love. Open and honest. How can I deny him?

"I love you, Cash." Please don't break my heart.

"I love you, too, Indigo. If it takes me the rest of my life, I'll prove to you I'm not going anywhere."

I trail a finger down his arm. "You could start now."

"I plan to."

His lips meet mine and I forget all about my fear of him leaving me behind. My fear of him realizing I don't fit into his rockstar life.

Chapter 29

Dream – Everything you've ever wanted

CASH

"Get up, Indy."

I shake her shoulder and she bats me away. "Go away."

"It's time to get up."

She burrows into her pillow. "No school today."

"Don't you want to come to the studio with me?"

She opens her eyes to glare at me. "I want to sleep in."

I waggle my eyebrows. "I'll make it worth your while."

She groans. "I'm too sore for you to make it worth my while."

I frown. Why didn't she say she was sore? I wouldn't have woken her in the middle of the night for another bout of sex had I known. I start for the hallway. "I'll run you a bath."

"Stop!" she shouts. "I don't need a bath. I need sleep."

"But I want you to come to the studio with me. I want you to see for yourself what we do. How normal we are."

"Because recording an album is normal?" she grumbles.

"I didn't want to do this…"

She narrows her eyes on me. "What?"

I pounce on the bed to tickle her. She squirms underneath me as she tries to escape.

"Stop! Stop! I'll go with you."

I smile down at her. "I love you."

Her hazel eyes warm until the green overtakes the blue and brown. "And I love you."

I bend over to reach her lips. She meets me halfway and our mouths meld together. I lick her seam before pushing my tongue inside. Her tongue meets mine and we duel for supremacy.

I growl before threading my hands through her hair and letting her know who's in charge. She sighs in surrender. My cock hardens. There's nothing sexier than Indy giving herself over to me.

I press my length against her stomach and she curls her legs around me to rub herself against my cock.

I yank my mouth away and push up to my elbows. "Shit. I'm sorry. You said you were sore. I'm an asshole."

"You're not an asshole. I'm simply irresistible."

I kiss her nose. "That you are," I say before rolling out of bed. "And now you're awake and can come to the studio with me."

"Are you sure you're a rockstar and not an evil mastermind?"

"Why can't I be both?"

She giggles as she sits up. "I guess I'm going to the studio."

"I'll wait for you downstairs."

"Don't make breakfast."

"You start a fire one time," I grumble.

Thirty minutes later, we're on our way to *Bertie's Recording Studio*. We hold hands as we walk since I can't be around Indy and not touch her.

We pass a store named *Sensual Scents* and Petal rushes outside.

"Good morning," Indy greets.

Petal wrings her hands. "I'm so sorry."

"Sorry? What are you sorry about?" I scan Main Street for a clue, but the small town is sleepy this morning.

"I should have delivered your candles last week, but I screwed up a batch."

"I didn't order any candles." Indy glances up at me.

I shrug. "Me either."

Petal ignores our responses. "How are you supposed to do wax play without candles?"

Indy's eyes widen. "Whoa. Wax play?"

"It's settled then." Petal nods. "No wax play for Indigo and Cash. I'll have massage candles sent over."

"Massage candles?" Indy asks.

"Don't worry. They're safe for use on all body parts."

Indy's mouth drops open. "All body parts?"

Petal's lips purse. "No wax play *and* no sexual massages? What do you do in the bedroom?"

I've had a lot of strange encounters as a musician – numerous requests to pet snakes or body parts and then there was the time a famous photographer wanted me to pose nude while urinating – but never in my life have I encountered a woman old enough to be my grandmother who openly disapproved of my choices in the bedroom.

"Don't worry, darling." I wink. "I can please my woman just fine without any candles."

Petal crosses her arms over her chest and raises her eyebrows at Indy whose cheeks flush in response.

"Yeah, um… we're good."

Indy tugs on my hand. I debate sticking around for a while and teasing her more but she's embarrassed. Teasing is okay. Embarrassing my girl is not.

"We need to get going."

"Off you go." Petal motions to the studio down the road. "Work on your album. I've been waiting for your next song to release."

"You listen to *Cash & the Sinners*?"

"Naturally, young man. I'm old. Not deaf." She scurries into her store without another word.

"Did we just have a conversation about our sex life with an elderly woman or am I still sleeping?" Indy asks as we continue toward the recording studio.

I chuckle. "I love this town."

"Good. Because you're stuck here for at least a year."

The words sound confident, but I know Indy's still worried about our future together. She thinks I can't settle down and is worried I travel too much. What she doesn't realize is I'd give it all up in a second for her. Fame isn't real. She is.

We reach the studio and I usher her inside.

"Hi, Indigo." Jett waves as he runs past.

"Hi, Indigo," Gibson greets as he chases Jett.

"What did Jett do now?" I ask Dylan.

He shrugs. "No idea."

Fender grunts from his position next to Dylan on the sofas.

"Fender doesn't know either," Dylan says.

"Can you interpret Fender's grunts?" Indy asks.

"You figure it out when you're around him enough."

"I can talk," Fender grumbles.

"But he prefers not to," I say.

Jett races toward us and stops in front of Indy before dropping to his knee. "Fair maiden, will you marry me?"

He reaches for her but I slap his hand away. "Knock it off. You're not funny."

Gibson raises his hand behind him. "I thought it was funny."

Jett's eyes widen in feigned surprise. "You do have a sense of humor?"

Gibson growls. "Scaring the shit out of someone isn't funny."

Jett laughs. "Yeah, it was."

Gibson steps toward Jett, but I shove my way between them. "Enough. We're supposed to be recording a song today."

"Are you staying, Indigo?" Dylan asks.

Indy bites her lip. "If you don't mind."

"Why would we mind? You're one of us now," he says and everyone nods in agreement.

I wrap my arm around her shoulder. "Welcome to the family, sweetness."

Our producer walks into the reception area. "Are we going to start at some time today?"

"This is Stan. He's our producer. This is my Indy," I introduce.

Indy smiles and waves at him.

"Great. A groupie. Just what we need."

Before I can respond, the band is lined up in front of Stan.

"She's one of us," Dylan insists, and Fender grunts in agreement.

"This is Indigo, you dumb shit," Jett says.

"Dumb shit," Gibson repeats.

Stan sighs and raises his hands in surrender. "Fine. Whatever. Are we making music today or what?"

"Let's go guys," I say and make my way toward the studio. I open the door to the sound room and motion toward our studio engineer. "This is Rob. You can stay in here with him."

I wait for Rob to be an asshole but he smiles at Indy and points to the sofa. "You can sit there."

Indy glances around. "You sure I won't be in the way?"

"You can never be in the way."

"Okay." She pushes up on her tiptoes to kiss me before making her way to the sofa. "Go make music."

I follow the guys into the studio. I sit on a stool in front of a microphone and pick up my guitar.

"What song are we doing today?" Stan asks over the microphone.

"Dreams." I want to sing this song to Indy. For her to know how much she means to me.

"You finished up the chorus?" Dylan asks.

"It could use some work."

Jett taps a rhythm out on his drums. "Let's hear it then."

I put on my headphones and find Indy. I hold her gaze as I sing.

"Love's a wild hurricane, refusing to conform,

In the chaos of life, it takes on any storm.

You were the missing chord, the rhythm in my soul,

In this crazy world, you made me feel whole."

"The first two lines are a bit corny," Dylan says when I stop singing.

"I like the last two lines," Jett says.

Gibson nods. "The last two lines are solid."

Fender grunts in agreement.

Great. Everyone thinks I should delete two lines of my chorus. I know they're not great, but they're not horrible, or are they?

"What do you think, Indy?"

Her eyes widen and she shakes her head. She speaks but I can't hear her.

"You have to use the mic."

Rob motions her over but she holds up her hands.

"Indy, come on."

She scowls at me as she stomps to the mic.

"I'm not a musician."

I smirk. "I've heard you sing in the shower. I know you're not a musician."

"Not helping your case," Dylan mutters.

He doesn't know Indy the way I do. Sometimes she needs a push.

She huffs. "The first two verses sound cliché."

"Thanks, sweetness." I smile at her. "I guess we're cutting the first two verses. Anyone have ideas for the lyrics?"

We get into our usual rhythm of bouncing ideas back and forth. I don't notice time passing until Indy enters the studio carrying bags of food. My stomach rumbles in response.

"What time is it?"

"After two," she says as she hands out the food.

"What do you think of the chorus now?" I ask.

"Sing it to me. I missed the last version while I was out picking up the food."

I take her hands and draw her near until she's standing between my legs.

"We danced through the fire,
And when the world got loud,
And the crowd got rough,
Your love was my shelter."

Her eyes warm as I sing to her. "It's good."

"Good enough for a *Cash & the Sinners* song?"

"Ask the guys."

I squeeze her hands. "I'm asking you."

"I think you forgot I teach fourth grade."

"I wish Indigo had been my fourth-grade teacher," Gibson says and I flip him off behind my back. "What? I bet she's a wonderful teacher. Way better than Mr. Burns."

"Your fourth-grade teacher wasn't Mr. Burns," Jett says.

Gibson shrugs. "He could have been. He had a hooked nose and slicked back gray hair."

I tune out Jett and Gibson's bickering.

"Told you we're normal," I whisper to Indy.

She raises her eyebrows. "This is normal?"

I bark out a laugh. "Love you, my Indy girl."

"Ah, Cash loves Indigo."

"Cash and Indigo sitting in a tree."

I bury my face in Indigo's neck as she laughs at my band's teasing. This right here is what I've always wanted. What I've always dreamed of. There's a reason I named the song about her dreams after all.

Chapter 30

Oblivious – When you fail to open your eyes and see what's right in front of you

Indigo

"Thanks for agreeing to help," Virginia greets when she opens her door. She notices the crowd behind me and scowls. "I didn't realize you were bringing *him* with you."

"Who's she referring to?" Gibson scans the group. "It's me, isn't it?"

He swaggers forward, but Jett shoves him out of the way. "I call dibs."

"You can't call dibs on a woman," I insist.

Jett scratches his chin. "You can't?"

"No, you can't," I repeat.

"But we can't share all the women," Gibson says.

"Wow." My eyes widen. "I don't even know where to begin with the two of you."

"Don't worry, darling. I know where to begin." Gibson winks.

Cash smacks him upside the head. "Knock it off before I shove you off of this porch."

"Nobody better harm my rose bushes," a woman shouts from inside the house.

Virginia sighs. "Your rose bushes are safe, Gratitude."

"Are you going to stand on my porch all day? I thought you were moving out today."

"I am moving out. I'll be out of your hair soon."

"Is that Gratitude the librarian? You live with your boss?" Dylan asks.

She glares at him. "I'm moving out. Or did you forget why you're here? Did syphilis rot your brain?"

"Syphilis? Does syphilis still exist?"

"As much fun as this is," I interrupt. "Let's get you moved."

Virginia motions to the boxes stacked in the hallway. "This is my stuff."

"What about your furniture?"

"I didn't bring any when I moved here. The apartment's furnished anyway."

It doesn't take long before the boxes are stacked in the truck.

"One more thing," Virginia calls before rushing into the house. She returns with a cage.

Gibson points at the small creature inside the cage. "What the hell is that thing?"

"Let me see." Jett sticks his finger in the cage. "Hey there, what's your name?" He yelps. "It bit me!"

Virginia rolls her eyes. "Didn't anyone ever teach you to not stick your finger where it doesn't belong?"

Jett waggles his eyebrows. "I've never had any complaints before."

Her cheeks flush. "Um… ah…," she stammers.

Dylan pushes him. "Don't embarrass, Virginia, asshole."

"I don't need you to protect me," she mumbles.

"Come on, Virginia." I herd her toward the truck. "We'll ride to the apartment. The rest of these jerks can walk."

"I'm not a jerk," Dylan proclaims.

"Just an idiot with severe memory loss," Virginia whispers so only I can hear her.

I bite my tongue to stop my laugh from spilling out. I'm not in any hurry for Dylan to figure out who Virginia is. I'm having entirely too much fun watching him spin his wheels.

"Are you excited about having your own place?" I ask once we're driving toward her apartment.

"Yeah. Living with your boss isn't fun."

I shiver. "Especially when your boss isn't exactly friendly."

She shrugs. "Gratitude isn't too bad."

"You obviously haven't had to deal with her after you returned a book a day late."

She gasps. "Indigo! You should know better."

I giggle. I've never returned a book late in my life, but teasing Virginia the righteous librarian is too much fun.

We pull into the parking lot of the apartment building. By the time Cash backs the truck up so we can easily unload, his bandmates are arriving.

"I win! I was here first," Jett declares.

Fender shoves him. "Not a race."

"Life is a race, dude. Get with the program."

Virginia groans. "You had to bring them to help me move?"

I smile. "They're fun."

"You have a strange way of saying annoying."

"You go ahead and unlock your new place," I nudge her toward the front door. "I'll deal with the hooligans."

"Okay. I'm on the second floor. Apartment 203."

I prop open the front door while the guys pick up boxes and begin carrying them inside.

"I'm going to tear down Virginia's walls since we're now neighbors," Dylan declares as he passes me.

"Don't be a jerk."

He grins. "This is going to be fun."

"Be nice to my friend," I call after him.

"I'm always nice."

"I'm not," Jett says. "But I am always fun."

"Stop bragging and get going or are your wimpy arms tired already?" Gibson goats.

"I'll show you tired."

Jett begins running up the stairs while holding the box above his head. Gibson is hot on his heels.

"Drop any of Virginia's stuff and you're answering to me!" Fender grunts next to me. "And to Fender!"

It only takes three trips before all of the boxes are unloaded. I collapse on the sofa next to Virginia who's cuddling a small animal to her chest.

"What ya got there?"

She smiles. "This is Harry, the hedgehog."

"Can I cuddle him?" I reach for him but she scoots away.

"Harry doesn't enjoy other people cuddling him."

"No shit. He bit my finger," Jett grumbles.

"And you enjoyed it," Gibson claims.

Jett smirks. "I always enjoy it a bit rough."

Dylan slaps him upside the head. "No sex talk in front of the ladies."

Virginia glares at Dylan. I wait for her to say something – to yell at him for speaking on her behalf – but she doesn't say anything.

"How did Harry come into your life?" I ask when silence falls.

"I found him on my driveway when I came home from work one night. He was injured. I rushed him to the vet and nursed him back to health." She smiles down at the little hedgehog.

"Can I pet him?" Dylan asks.

Virginia shakes her head. "He's scared of strangers."

He frowns down at her but steps away without pushing the point. "Is anyone thirsty?"

Virginia ducks her chin. "I haven't had a chance to do groceries yet."

"No worries. I'll grab stuff from my place."

Her nose scrunches. "Your place?"

"Yeah. My place." He points to the apartment across the hallway. "I live there."

"You live across from me?"

He grins. "Yep. Didn't you know your new apartment used to be Gibson and Fender's apartment?"

She rears back. "No, I didn't."

She appears horrified. And now I feel bad. I assumed she knew Gibson and Fender used to live here. The whole town knows Gibson, Fender, and Jett rented a house together. Dylan claimed he didn't want to live somewhere with a revolving door of women, but I'm beginning to think he wanted to stay here to be across the hallway from Virginia.

"Don't worry. We bought you new mattresses," Gibson says.

Fender grunts. "My mattress was fine."

"Because you're a monk."

"I'm not a monk."

"Oh, do you prefer the term celibate?"

Fender growls. "Not fucking every woman who throws herself at me doesn't mean I'm celibate."

Gibson scratches his neck. "It doesn't?"

"In case anyone's wondering, I don't have sex with every woman who throws herself at me either," Dylan declares.

I bite my tongue before I laugh at him. Could he be more obvious? And completely oblivious? Steam pours from Virginia's ears every time he makes a pass at her. And, yet, he hasn't bothered to try and figure out why.

"Me either." Cash plops down on the sofa next to me. "I'm a one woman man."

Jett coughs. "Whipped."

Cash wraps an arm around my shoulders and draws me near. "I don't care what your dumbass thinks."

I cuddle into his hold. I try not to care what Jett thinks either but I can't help but wonder. Will Cash regret being with me? Will he be bored with me when he can have a smorgasbord of women while on tour?

I force those thoughts from my mind. I'm not going to question whether I can trust Cash all the time. I need to have faith in him and his love for me.

I inhale a deep breath.

Have faith, Indy. Have faith.

Chapter 31

Love – If it comes with strings attached it isn't worth a damn

Indigo

The doorbell rings and I groan. "Can't we have one day to sleep in?"

Cash buries his face in my neck. "Apparently not."

"If it's your bandmates, I'm going to kill them."

He chuckles. "It's cute you think they'd ring the bell."

The doorbell rings again. "Whoever it is, is impatient."

He sighs. "I'll go."

"You got home after three from the recording studio. Stay in bed," I insist.

"If you're sure."

I kiss his cheek. "I'm sure."

I snatch Cash's hoodie from the floor and put it on over my pajamas.

The doorbell rings yet again.

"Geez. Hold your horses," I mutter as I shut the bedroom door behind me and hurry down the stairs to the front door.

"Good…." My greeting trails off when I notice who's at the door. "Mom. What are you doing here?"

"Is that any way to greet your mother?"

She can't bother to say hello before beginning to criticize me?

"Won't you come in?" I swing the door open wide and motion her inside.

Mom glances around the hallway and living room as I lead her toward the kitchen. I need coffee if I'm going to survive a surprise visit from my mother.

"Have a seat. I'll make some coffee."

She checks her watch. "There's no time."

"No time? Where are you going?"

"I think you mean where are *we* going."

I give up on the coffee and whirl around to face her. "Okay. I'll bite. Where are we going?"

"We're ..." She scowls. "What are you wearing?"

"Pajamas."

"Pajamas?"

Geez. I'm glad I didn't wake up naked the way I do most mornings after Cash spent the night in my bed. But he got home late last night and passed out before I had a chance to seduce him.

"It's what most people sleep in."

"Don't be condescending toward me. I'm referring to your sweatshirt."

Uh oh. Is Cash's sweatshirt offensive? I didn't bother looking at it before putting it on. But it's just a simple *Cash & the Sinners* concert sweatshirt. Nothing offensive here. Unless you're my mother and hate rock and roll.

"It's a band," I explain.

She purses his lips. "I know it's a band. I also know whose band it is."

Darn. I was hoping to avoid this conversation for another twenty years or so. I figure once Cash and I give Mom a few grandkids, she'll settle down. But since she brought it up, I can't let it go.

"Never mind. We'll let bygones be bygones. Get your stuff," she says before I have a chance to figure out how to start a discussion about what she did to me and Cash.

"Get my stuff?"

"Yes, Indigo, get your stuff."

"Why?"

"Don't be daft. I'm taking you home."

I open my arms to indicate the house. "I am home."

She scowls. "I will not allow you to live in Saffron's house."

I rear back. "Allow me? Since when do you allow me to do anything? I'm twenty-nine. I'm a grown woman."

"You're not acting very grown now, are you?"

"What are you talking about?"

She sighs. "I really hoped we could avoid doing this."

"I don't even know what *this* is."

I must be sleeping because this cannot be happening. My mom did not show up in Winter Falls to drag me back home because she doesn't approve of my life choices. I hope Cash wakes me up soon. This dream sucks.

"I don't know why you insist on defying me."

I inhale a deep breath in a search for calm. It doesn't work, so I try again. After three breaths, I give up. There is no calm to be found. Mom really should have let me drink a cup of coffee before starting in on me.

"I'm not defying you, Mom. I'm simply living my own life."

"You're making a mistake is what you're doing."

Dare I ask? Yes, I do. "What mistake am I making?"

"She's referring to me," Cash says as he enters the room. He comes to stand next to me and I grasp his hand for support.

Mom slams her purse onto the kitchen table. "After everything I did to save you from this man, you're sneaking around with him yet again."

Save me from Cash? Is she crazy? Her idea of saving me nearly destroyed me. "We're not sneaking around."

"Why else are you hiding in Winter Falls?"

"If you would have shown up at Grandma's funeral then—"

She raises a palm to stop me. "I will not have my daughter criticize my decisions."

"Must be nice," I mutter.

Mom points to me. "Don't you dare backtalk me, Indigo Scott."

I sigh. "What do you want, Mom? Why are you here?"

"Once again, you're not listening. I'm here to take you home and get you away from that heathen."

I growl. "You better not be referring to Cash as a heathen."

She tilts her nose in the air. "He is a heathen."

"Could you please stop referring to my boyfriend as a nasty word?"

"Your boyfriend?" She scowls. "It's worse than I thought. You've fallen for his charm again. He's only going to hurt you again."

"No. He's not going to hurt me." I point to her. "You're the one who hurt me. You're the one who made him break up with me. You're the one who caused all my heartache. Not Cash."

She flips her hand in the air as if to dismiss my words. "He would have hurt you eventually. Like father like son."

Cash stiffens next to me. I squeeze his hand to let him know I'm on his side. I'll always be on his side.

"Bullshit."

Mom rears back at my use of profanity.

"Bullshit," I repeat. "Cash is not his father. Cash is his own man. A man I'm proud to know. A man I'm proud to stand next to."

Mom snorts. "Easy to say when the money is flowing from his career."

"What is wrong with you? I'm serious. I want to know. What in the world is wrong with you? Why do you throw nasty accusations at him? You don't even know him. You never took the time to get to know him. From the minute we started dating in high school, you were nasty. You didn't even try."

"Yes, well, I knew better than to waste my time."

"Waste your time? It's a waste of time to get to know your only daughter's boyfriend? It's a waste of time to be nice to someone you don't know? It's a waste of time to get to know me? Your only daughter?"

My breath hitches on the last words and Cash wraps his arms around me to hold me close.

"I can't believe you're being this stubborn. I blame your father."

I wrest out of Cash's arms and stomp toward my mother. "Don't you dare blame Dad for being a decent human being."

She checks her watch. "Can we continue this discussion later? We need to hurry if we're going to catch our plane."

I cross my arms over my chest. "I'm not going anywhere with you."

"Of course, you are. Now, get your things."

"I'm staying here with Cash."

Her eyes narrow. Thank goodness I became immune to those ice daggers long ago or I'd be bleeding out on the kitchen floor of Grandma's house.

"No, you are not."

"Yes, I am."

"You are not."

"I am, too."

"If you stay here with that man, I will never speak to you again."

"The same way you never spoke to Grandma after your fight with her?"

"Why do you think I never spoke to Saffron again?" She nods toward Cash. "It's all his fault."

Cash opens his mouth to speak but I stop him with a shake of my head. Raven is my mother. She's my burden to deal with.

He doesn't deal with her. Not if she can't learn to speak to him in a civilized manner.

"You fought with Grandma over Cash?"

Mom lets out a long-suffering sigh as if I'm the one who's being irrational and not her. "Saffron thought I was overstepping for telling Cash to break up with you."

"You didn't simply tell Cash to break up with me. You blackmailed him."

"It wasn't blackmail."

"What do you call it when you demand someone perform an act or else you'll hurt someone they love? I call it blackmail."

"You always were such a dramatic child."

I was no such thing. I wasn't allowed to be in her house. I had to be quiet and get good grades or else. Mom was always good at the 'or else' threat.

Wear this outfit or else…

Take this class or else…

Stop being friends with her or else…

And just like that.

I'm done.

I am done kowtowing to a woman who uses her love like a weapon. I am done trying to make her happy. I am done putting her first.

I am done trying to earn her love. I shouldn't have to earn my mother's love. It should be a given. Unconditional because I'm her child.

"Please leave."

"Excuse me?"

"You heard me." I point to the front door. "You should go now."

"I'm not going anywhere alone."

"Who do you think is going with you? Not me."

"This is ridiculous." She picks up her purse. "I'm warning you if you don't come with me now, I will never speak to you again."

"It's a hardship, but I think I can survive."

I will no longer allow her to attach threats and blackmail to her love. Love should be given free without any strings attached.

"Indy," Cash urges.

"Nope. I am not ending our relationship because my mother is too stuck up to realize how happy you make me."

Mom frowns. "Having a partnership is not about happiness."

I laugh. "I think Dad figured that out long ago." And why he stays with her is anybody's guess.

"Well, I never…"

"That's the problem. You never." Never consider anyone else's feelings. Never think about anyone other than herself. There's a lot she 'never' does.

I herd her toward the front door. "Thanks for stopping by." Not.

"You'll regret this, Indigo," she claims as she steps outside.

"I wouldn't hold your breath," I say before shutting the door on her.

Chapter 32

Goodbye – What you say when you're a yellow-bellied coward

CASH

As soon as the door closes behind her mother, Indy's shoulders slump. I want to hold her in my arms and comfort her, but I don't. I can't comfort her while doing what needs to be done.

"Maybe you should go after her."

She glares at me. Whereas her mother's glare makes me want to hide in a closet while covering my junk, Indy's glare makes my cock twitch. Inconvenient timing.

"Why the hell would I go after her after everything she said?"

I ignore her icy glare and place my hands on her shoulders. "Because she's your mom."

"She's also a bitch." Her eyes widen and she slaps a hand over her mouth.

Damn, she's cute when she swears. I kiss her nose before retreating a step.

"You're going to regret it if you don't go after her."

Her nostrils flare. "How can you say those words after everything she said about you? She stood here in this kitchen where we live together and bad-mouthed you. How dare she!"

I shove my hands in my pockets and shrug. "Maybe she's right."

She fast blinks. "I'm sorry. I think I'm having some kind of psychotic episode. You did not say my mother is right."

"Don't be cute."

"I'm not trying to be cute. I'm hoping I'm still asleep in bed with your arms wrapped around me and our legs tangled together."

Which is exactly where I want to be, too. But I don't deserve Indy. She's way too good for me. I forgot for a while but her mom reminded me all too well. I'm the bastard child who caused a rift between Indy's mom and grandmother.

"I'm serious, Indy. She's getting away."

She rears back. "She's getting away? Do you seriously expect me to chase her?"

"I don't want to drive a wedge between you and your mom."

I know how it feels to not have a mom. I don't want Indy to experience what I did.

"You're not. She is."

I scowl. "If it weren't for me, you wouldn't have had this argument."

She scoffs. "Are you kidding? She came here to drag me home."

"Because of me."

"No," she insists. "Because of Grandma. She's taking her frustration with Grandma out on me."

I run a hand along my jaw. Damn this is hard. I'd rather perform a concert completely naked with my junk on display than have this conversation.

"The argument between your mom and your grandma was about me."

She waves away my argument. "Mom and Grandma fought all the time."

"Maybe they did, but the fight that caused them to stop speaking to each other was about me." I tap my chest. "I'm the reason they didn't speak for over a decade. Me."

She steps toward me but I back away.

"No, Cash. No. If the fight hadn't been about you, it would have been about something else. You weren't the reason. You were the excuse."

She's wrong. I am the reason. This is all my fault.

I'm such an idiot. What made me think I could keep Indy? I don't deserve her. She's way too good for me. Something her mom will never let me forget.

"Maybe your mom is right. Maybe we should—"

Indy's growl cuts me off. "Don't you dare finish that sentence."

"It's true. I'm not good enough for you."

"Who says? Is there some scoreboard somewhere keeping track of who's good enough for whom I don't know about? Is there an app I need to download?"

"I'm being serious."

She pokes my chest. "So." Poke. "Am." Poke. "I."

I capture her hand. When I realize I'm drawing circles on her skin with my thumbs, I release her. I can't do what has to be done if I'm touching her. Feeling her skin. Feeling the electricity flowing between us like a live wire.

"It's my fault." I pause to swallow. I don't want to say this. I don't want to hurt Indy, but it needs to be said.

"What are you talking about now?"

"It's my fault your mom wasn't at Saffron's funeral."

She scowls. "No, it's Mom's fault for holding a grudge."

"It's my fault, Indy. If your Mom and Grandma hadn't had this big argument about me, your mom would have been at the funeral to support you."

"I didn't need her. I had you."

Her declaration makes me pause. Maybe she's right. Maybe I can fill the hole left by her mother. Maybe I can—

I press the heel of my palm against my heart where I feel an emptiness left by my mother dying. I'm kidding myself. I can't fill the hole the absence of her mother would cause in Indy.

"I can't do this."

"Can't do what?"

"I can't be the cause of a rift between you and your mom."

A muscle ticks in her jaw. "It's not your decision to make."

"Nonetheless." I'm making it.

"You're breaking up with me?" Her breath hitches and I fist my hands before I reach for her. It's not my place to comfort Indy now. I lost that privilege.

"It's for the best."

"The best for whom?" She points at herself. "Me?"

"Yes."

"Liar."

"I'm not—"

"This is your excuse. You got what you want. A roll in the hay with the old high school girlfriend but now your album is nearly done and you need an excuse to extricate yourself from the situation. And along comes Mom with an excuse wrapped up in a neat little bow for you."

"It's not an excuse."

She snorts. "What do you want to call it then? Cowardness? I can live with that."

"I'm not a coward."

"Bwak! Bwak! Sounds as if you are one to me."

"Indy, can you be serious for one minute, please?"

"Me?" She pounds a fist on her chest. "I'm the one who needs to be serious?"

Is this a trick question? "Yes?"

"How's this for serious?" She motions to the front entrance. "If you walk out the door, don't you ever come back here again."

A lump forms in my throat making speaking impossible. I nod instead.

"You can go off and be the famous rockstar. You don't have to worry about cheating on the poor, boring girlfriend back home. You can sleep with all the groupies you want."

I clench my jaw. "I am not breaking up with you because I want to fuck groupies."

She crosses her arms over her chest. "Sure, you aren't."

"Indy, listen to me." I reach for her but she bats me away. "Please try to understand."

"Understand what? How you're a coward? Or how you wield excuses to get your way?"

"You're not listening. I don't want to come between your mom and you. I want you to have your mom."

"There you go again – wielding excuses. You know darn well I barely speak to my mom."

I didn't.

"Tell me the real reason," she urges. "Tell me why you're being a complete jerk and breaking up with me."

Didn't she pay attention to anything her mom had to say? I'm not good enough for her. I'm a bastard child of an alcoholic. I grew up in a dirty dilapidated trailer with holes in the floor while she grew up in a cookie-cutter house with a white picket fence.

She had two parents who loved her. Who would do anything for her. I had one who used her money to buy alcohol instead of feeding her son. And one who refused to acknowledge my existence.

"You deserve better than me."

"You're the best thing to ever happen to me, Cash. I love you. You are everything to me. You're my heart. Please, don't break mine."

Her heart will heal. She'll find a good man. A man who can give her everything she's ever wanted. A man who's clean. Who isn't a bastard. A man who has a mom and dad who love him.

Who didn't grow up wearing donated clothes. Didn't grow up wondering where his next meal would come from.

While my heart will always belong to her. No matter what happens in my life, I'm hers. She won't be mine. She'll belong to another. But I will always be hers.

"Love isn't always enough."

She clutches my hands. "Of course, it is. Haven't you read the stories? Love conquers all."

"I wish it did, but stories are just stories."

"Don't make me beg."

I unwind her hands from mine and kiss her nose one last time. "I would never make you beg, Indy. You're a princess. You should beg no one."

A lone tear falls down her cheek. I want to brush it away. Brush all of her tears away.

I need to get the hell out of here before I cave. Before I allow her to convince me I'm wrong.

I'm not wrong. I'm not good enough for Indy.

"Goodbye, Indigo."

I walk out the front door. I don't look back. Not even when I hear her sob. I keep walking until the sound of her sobs fades. Until the pounding of my broken heart is all I hear.

Chapter 33

Stalking – What happens when a bunch of old women won't leave you alone

Indigo

The doorbell rings and I peek through the curtains in the living room to check who it is before opening the door. I made the mistake of not checking enough times today. Lesson finally learned.

Phew. It's Virginia.

I rush to the door and open it before grabbing her elbow to haul her inside. "Get in here."

"What's going on?" she asks as she wrests out of my grip.

"You-hoo! Indigo!" Petal hollers as she rushes across the street toward the house.

I push Virginia out of the way and shut the door as if I didn't hear Petal. For good measure, I lock the door. I don't trust those gossip gals to not break into my place.

"Away from the door." I usher Virginia to the kitchen where she sets down the bags of groceries she's carrying.

"Okay, now you really have to tell me what's happening."

"The gossip gals are stalking me."

Her eyes widen. "Stalking you? Do we need to call the police?"

I snort. "I don't need the police. I need someone to teach those women what the definition of privacy means."

"What did they do?"

"Every time I open my door they attack."

"Attack?"

"Rush me to ask me questions. Why was your mom here? What happened with Cash? Am I heartbroken?"

Of course, I'm heartbroken. The man I love dumped me because my mom is a bitch. How could I not be?

Tears well in my eyes but I sniff to stop them from falling down my face. I want to scream and shout. I want to cry my eyes out. But I inhale a deep breath and keep it all inside. Virginia would run straight into the arms of the gossip gals if let the heartbreak beast lose in this house.

"No wonder you asked me to bring you groceries."

"Exactly." I nod. "I wasn't facing the gossip gal firing squad again."

She shivers. "Those women scare me. The last time they came into the library, they got mad because they couldn't find some book they wanted and confronted Gratitude. They ended up in a screaming match with them yelling at her for being a prude because she didn't source books about BDSM."

She ducks her head but not before I notice her cheeks heat.

"I wish I had been there."

"I wish I hadn't."

I dig into the first bag and start emptying it. "Anyway, I didn't want to face them again, but I needed supplies." Heartbreak calls for chocolate, potato chips, and alcohol.

Virginia grasps my wrist to stop me. "I'm sorry about Cash. Can I ask what happened or will you kick me out?"

I would never kick Virginia out. She's my only friend in Winter Falls. I thought Cash and the band were my friends but Cash showed me his true colors today.

"He dumped me."

"Dumped you? That man loves you more than life. When he looks at you, he has cartoon hearts in his eyes."

"And yet...." I guess Cash had her fooled too. At least I'm not alone in believing Cash's lies.

"I'm sorry. What a dick." Her eyes widen at her choice of word.

My lips nearly turn up at how outraged she appears at her own behavior but not even Virginia's adorable shy behavior can bring a smile to my face today. "A total dick."

"Did he give you a reason?"

"He's not 'good enough for me'. Bull cocky," I snarl. "He wants to remain unattached so he can sleep with all his groupies when he goes back on tour. I was a fun distraction but now it's over."

"Do you honestly believe he broke up with you to sleep with other women?"

What other reason is there? None of what happened makes sense to me. Except for my mom being a witch. Her behavior was completely normal. As was her impromptu visit. Classic Mom move.

But I'm done with Mom's moves. No matter what my relationship status with Cash is, I'm done trying to earn her love. It's about time she starts trying to earn mine. And my love will not be easy to earn.

"Are we going for 'I hate him and want revenge' or 'I will love him forever and want to drown my sorrows in chocolate'?"

I stare at her. Where's the shy librarian Virginia I know and love?

"What? I can do revenge."

Bless her heart. She's offering me a distraction. I'll take it.

"This I gotta hear. Tell me more."

"We can print out a picture of his face and throw darts at it."

"Good idea but I don't have any darts and if I remember junior year of high school correctly neither one of us is talented at throwing things."

She winces. "What was the gym teacher thinking?"

"I don't want to have to replace the windows."

"Dart throwing is out. Got it." She taps her chin. "We can troll him on social media. Say he has a tiny you-know-what."

"He doesn't check his social media. Besides, half the world has slept with him. They know the truth."

A memory of Dylan teasing Cash about how few women he's slept with tries to push to the forefront of my mind, but I won't let it. I'm not going to spend the day analyzing every little thing Cash and his friends said and did. That path leads to madness.

"How about a voodoo doll? We can make one of him and stick pins in it."

My eyes widen. "Voodoo dolls? What do you know about voodoo dolls?"

"Gratitude's Wi-Fi didn't always work. This one time when I ran out of books to read on my Kindle, I plundered her bookshelf and found a book on voodoo."

"Gratitude had a book on voodoo?"

Virginia shrugs. "It was all things voodoo or a book on the history of salt."

"I don't think we have the supplies to make voodoo dolls. Any other ideas?"

She shakes her head.

"I guess revenge is out."

She rifles in one of the bags and brings out a bottle of wine. "Drown your sorrows?"

Now, we're talking. I hold out my hand. "I don't need a glass."

Her nose wrinkles. "Ew. I do."

She pours me a glass and hands it to me before returning to emptying the bags. She pulls out various chocolate bars, another bottle of wine, a bottle of tequila, a few bags of chips, and a pizza.

"We'll have the pizza for lunch," she says as she places it in the refrigerator.

"Lunch?" I check the clock. It's only ten a.m. "Oh no. I didn't think. Do you need to get to the library?"

"I'm taking a personal day."

"You don't need to do that."

She picks up her wine and sits down next to me. "And you didn't have to chase those bullies away."

"They tripped you and made you drop all your books. Of course, I chased them away."

She lifts her wine glass. "Of course, I took a personal day."

We chink glasses before I take a large gulp of my wine. To her credit, she doesn't say anything about my day drinking. She merely stands and grabs a bag of chips.

We move to the living room sofa where we drink our wine in silence. I manage to hold back the tears until the second glass.

"I can't believe Cash." I sniffle. "I told him I loved him and he walked away."

Virginia wraps an arm around me and I lay my head on her shoulder.

"I'm sorry."

I swipe at the tears flowing down my face. "He doesn't want to drive a wedge between me and my mom." I snort. "Mom drove a wedge all on her own when she blackmailed him into breaking up with me at our high school graduation."

"I always wondered why you two split after high school."

"Because my mom's a horrible person and he's a coward."

She hums. "I wouldn't say coward."

I lean back to scowl at her. "Don't tell me you're on Cash's side."

She raises her arms in the air. "I'm on your side, Indigo. Always."

"Good," I mutter.

"What is it with men and throwing it all away for fame?"

"Do you mean Dylan?"

"Dylan's a jerk."

"Are you ever going to tell him why you won't go out with him?

"Are you kidding? And miss watching his dumb face go all confused because I don't fall at his feet? No way."

"Dumb face." I giggle. "At least, we have each other."

It will always only be each other since I will never find a man to love the way I love Cash. My chance at happiness - at a husband and family walked out my door this morning – and he isn't coming back.

My heart clenches and breathing becomes difficult. I gasp. "He broke my heart."

Virginia rubs circles on my back. "Let it go, Indigo. Let it all out."

And I do. My heart cracks open and all the pain and hurt I'm feeling tumble out. I curl into a ball on the sofa to keep my insides from spilling out as the tears fall down my face. Until the upholstery is wet with my tears. Until I can no longer handle the pain and pass out.

Chapter 34

Truth or Punch – The game you play when you fucked up your life

CASH

There's a knock on the door and Dylan sighs before standing to answer it. My ears perk up as I listen for who's here. Maybe it's Indy. Maybe she's returned to me.

"Your family's here," Dylan announces as he leads my brothers into the living room.

"What are you guys doing here?" It's the middle of the day. Shouldn't they be working?

"It's time," Miller declares.

"Time for what?"

Brody slams a bottle of tequila on the coffee table. "For truth or punch."

"I have no idea what you're talking about, and I don't drink hard liquor."

"Because your mom was an alcoholic?" Brody asks.

Riley elbows him. "Way to be sensitive."

"I've got beer." Dylan grabs a six-pack and sets it on the coffee table. "You good?"

No, I'm not good. The woman I love is not in my arms. I will never be good again.

"Message if you need anything." He saunters off and I'm left with my family.

I nod to the tequila. "What's going on?"

Damon sits on the sofa next to me. "We have this tradition."

"For when a brother fucks up," Riley says.

"And you fucked up, dude," Brody says.

"Do they always parrot each other?" I ask the group.

Elder chuckles. "Welcome to a family of twins."

Peace clears his throat. "We're not a family of twins anymore."

Riley smirks. "There are still four of us and only three of you."

Brody holds up his hand and the two high-five. "We win."

Elder rubs his hands together. "What did the drummer name his twins?" He laughs before continuing, "Anna One and Anna Two."

I snort. Damon elbows me. "Don't encourage him. You'll make him think he's funny."

Elder puffs out his chest. "I am funny."

Miller grunts. "Are we going to do this or are we going to gossip like old ladies?"

I hold up my hands. "I don't know what we're doing."

Brody grins. "Truth or punch."

"Don't you mean truth or dare?"

"Nope."

I look to Damon for an answer. He seems to be the most reasonable of this group. Other than Peace, but he's a cop, and – brother or not – I don't ask cops questions.

"It's this game we play whenever a Bragg brother screws up."

"I'm not a Bragg brother," I'm quick to point out.

"Dude," is all Miller says but everyone nods in agreement.

Damon continues as if I hadn't interrupted him. "We ask you questions. You have to answer with the truth or get punched by whoever asked the question."

Get punched? And here I thought I wanted to have a bunch of siblings who care about me.

"And you have to down a shot for every question regardless of whether you tell the truth or get punched," Elder adds.

"I don't drink shots."

I'm firm on this. Have I gotten drunk in the past? Sure, I'm not a teetotaler. But I stay away from hard liquor and usually stick to two or three bottles of beer max. I have no desire to become my mother.

"You can substitute beer for the hard liquor," Damon concedes.

Brody swipes the bottle from the table. "More tequila for me!"

Peace yanks the tequila from his hands. "No tequila for you."

Brody sticks out his bottom lip and pouts. "But I love tequila."

"Isn't your girlfriend about to have a baby? Maybe you want to stay sober in case she goes into labor?" I ask.

Brody sighs. "Having a rockstar in the family is not as fun as I expected."

"Fame isn't real," I tell him.

"Is that why you broke up with Indigo? Because you're famous?" Peace asks.

"Um…"

He nods toward the beer. "You have to drink no matter what."

"I don't want to get drunk," I grumble but I open a bottle and swig from it.

Damon bumps my shoulder. "Now, answer the question or Peace gets to punch you."

I size Peace up. He's in shape. As he should be since he's a police officer. But I'm not a pushover. Running around a stage for two hours while singing requires stamina. Stamina I've gained with a running and gym routine. I could handle a punch from him.

But this is an easy question. I'll save the fights for the hard ones.

"I didn't break up with Indy because I'm famous, although she believes my fame is the problem."

I barely finish my response before Damon asks, "Why does Indigo think your fame is a problem?"

I scowl at him. He nods toward the beer bottle in my hand. I sip on my beer as I consider my response.

"She thinks I dumped her in high school to become a rockstar."

"Did you?" Elder asks.

"No."

"Why did you dump Indigo?" Miller asks.

I narrow my eyes on him as I drink from my beer. I'm not stupid. I know this is the question they want to know the answer to. But I'm at a loss as to how much to tell them. I'm not used to having siblings who ask questions and demand answers.

"She deserves better than me."

Riley smirks. "Why did you tell Indigo you broke up with her?" I glare at him. He couldn't accept my non-answer as an answer? "This isn't the first time we've played this little game."

"Great. Something to look forward to."

"Except you won't be in Winter Falls for long," Brody says and I switch my glare to him. "What? Am I wrong?"

"No." I would have stayed but … I blow out a breath. No sense thinking about what could have been.

"My turn," Peace begins but Riley cuts him off.

"Nu-uh. He hasn't answered my question yet."

Crap. I thought I got away with avoiding his question. Guess not.

"I told Indigo she deserved better than me."

Everyone groans at my response.

"Does your breaking up with Indigo have something to do with her mother's arrival in town?" Peace asks.

"How do you know Raven was here?"

He rolls his eyes. "Welcome to small town living in Winter Falls."

"Except he's not staying," Damon says.

"Answer the question," Miller grumbles.

"Geez. Who pissed in your Cheerios?"

"He and Eden are trying for a baby. He wants to get home to 'work' on the situation," Elder explains.

I thought Indy and I were headed toward babies and white picket fences and I do's. Instead, I'm sleeping on my bandmate's couch. Life sucks.

Peace kicks my foot. "Answer the question. Did you break up with Indigo because of anything her mom said or did?"

I shrug. "Kind of."

Brody presses a fresh bottle of beer in my hands. "Drink."

"Kind of is not an accepted answer," Peace explains. "You can correct your answer or I'll punch you." He appears excited about the prospect of punching me. Great. Something to look forward to.

"Raven pointed out how I will never be good enough for Indy."

"What the actual hell?" Damon asks.

"It's true." I slump against the sofa. "I'm a bastard with an alcoholic mother."

He grits his teeth and a muscle in his jaw ticks. "Is my daughter less than because her biological mother abandoned her?"

I rear back. "No. Of course not."

"Do you think I'm a bastard?" Peace asks.

"Um, no."

"Damon Bragg, Sr., never acknowledged my existence either."

I wave away his answer. "Your situation is different. You were raised by two loving parents. I'm trailer trash."

"I really want to punch some sense into you," Peace says.

Miller grunts. "I got this."

He prowls toward me and I slide down the sofa until I'm practically sitting on Damon's lap. "I'm answering all of your questions."

"But you're being a dumbass," Riley says.

"And this is from the man who needed three second chances from Moon," Brody points out.

Riley punches Brody in the shoulder but before Brody can respond, Peace steps between them. "Enough. We have bigger problems to deal with than your identical twin bullshit."

"I'm not a problem. I solved the problem," I claim. "I let Indy go."

"You let the woman you love go because you're an idiot. Not sure how this solved a problem," Damon claims.

"I'm not an idiot."

"Would you think less of me because I grew up in a trailer?" Peace asks.

"Of course not."

"Do you think Indigo thinks less of you because you grew up in a trailer?"

"She begged me not to leave." I slam my eyes shut as the memory assails me.

"Then, why do you think you're not good enough for her?"

Remind me never to go up against my interrogator half-brother again. I didn't want to tell him any of this and yet I find myself spilling my secrets to all of my brothers.

"Say I'm good enough for her," I begin. Damn them for making some good points about my past.

"Hold up!" Damon raises his hand. "You are good enough for her."

"Yeah," Peace nods in agreement. "Growing up in a trailer doesn't make you less than. It's not your fault your mother was an alcoholic. And it definitely isn't your fault your father was an asshole who didn't bother to get to know you."

"Being a good man has nothing to do with who your father is," Miller grumbles. "It's *your* actions and *your* deeds that determine *your* worth. Not whose name is on your birth certificate."

I contemplate what he's saying. I would never judge anyone for having an asshole for a dad. Why then am I being harsh on myself?

Raven. Indy's mom never fails to make me feel less than. But she's only one person. A person who couldn't be bothered to show up at her mother's funeral. Maybe her opinion isn't important.

Crap. Did I screw up?

"Okay." I nod to concede his point. "But what about the future? I'm still on the road for more than half the year. I won't be home to run her a bath when she has a bad day."

"Do you have access to phones on the road?" Brody asks.

What kind of question is this? "Yeah."

"Then you phone her or Facetime her. Modern technology is pretty cool." He winks.

"Next issue," Damon demands.

"Indy hates how famous I am."

"She does? Has she told you as much?" he asks.

I scowl. "No, but she worries about all the groupies who throw themselves at me because of my fame."

"Then, prove to her that being famous won't affect your relationship." He makes it sound simple. It's anything but.

"How?"

Brody rubs his hands together. "I have a few ideas."

Everyone groans.

Peace points at him. "Nothing illegal."

Brody bats his eyelashes. "Naturally."

"Let's hear this," I say because I think they might be right. I think I screwed up. I let Indy's mom get into my head and mess me up.

Indy still may deserve a better man than me – one who grew up with a loving family and didn't spend his childhood scrounging for food – but I'm going to do everything in my power to make sure she never regrets being with me.

Just as soon as I convince her to give me another chance.

Chapter 35

Grand gesture – What happens when someone realizes he was a dumbass and needs to apologize in a big way

Indigo

Knock! Knock!

At the knock on the door, I bury my head under my blanket. I'm not ready to face the world yet. Things I never thought I'd be grateful for: the love of my life breaking up with me on the eve of a long weekend so I could wallow for three days before going back to school.

"Indigo! I know you're in there," Dylan hollers.

"Go away!"

"I'm not going anywhere until you let me in."

I guess he'll be sleeping on the porch.

"The old lady across the street has her binoculars pointed at this house."

Petal can use her binoculars all she wants. She won't observe anything exciting since I'm not moving from my position on the couch. Never mind how the stuffing is lacking and the coils are pinching my back. I'm not moving.

"I guess I'll have to give her a show."

I expect him to play his guitar but all I hear is humming. I listen closer. Is he humming *Blurred Lines*? Why is he humming *Blurred Lines*? Do I want to know?

I wrap the blanket around me and stand. I wobble for a moment since lying on the sofa crying for two days doesn't exactly add muscle tone to your legs. Once my feet are steady, I inch toward the window and peek outside.

Dylan has his shirt off and he's whirling it in the air.

"What are you doing?"

"Giving your neighbors a show!"

He reaches for the snap of his jeans, and I rush to the front door and yank it open before shackling Dylan's wrist and dragging him inside. It's not difficult since he doesn't put up a fight. In fact, he smirks. Dang it to detention and back! He got exactly what he wanted.

"Why are you here?" I snarl at him.

He rakes his gaze up and down my body. I tighten the blanket around my waist.

"You'll need to change." He sniffs. "And take a shower." He points to my hair. "And wash your hair."

"What are you talking about?"

"Good thing I got here early."

Gee. His response cleared things up. Not. I try again. "What are you talking about?"

He smirks. "We're going out."

I scoot backwards. "No, we're not. I have another day off before classes begin again. I'm not going anywhere before then."

"Huh." He studies me with a frown on his face, but all he says is 'huh'. Annoying.

"What?"

"I didn't expect *the* Indigo Scott to be a scaredy-cat."

"I'm not *the* Indigo Scott. I'm Indigo. And I'm not a scaredy-cat."

"I don't know." He nods toward the coffee table and the ruins of my heartbreak meal. "It sure seems like you're a scaredy-cat who's afraid to leave her house."

"I'm not afraid. I don't want to go anywhere. There's a difference."

Katy Purry strolls into the entryway and plops down beside me. She licks her front paws while contemplating Dylan.

I expect him to skedaddle. Katy Purry has frightened off bigger men than him.

What I don't expect is for Dylan to kneel in front of my kitty and motion her toward him. What I double don't expect is for Katy Purry to stroll to him and for Dylan to pick her up and cradle her in his arms.

"Who's a pretty kitty?" he coos to her.

I expect Katy Purry to swipe at him but her eyes fall shut and she revels in his attention.

"Go shower. I'll feed your kitty."

"I'm not showering."

His nose scrunches. "Your choice but I would put on a different outfit."

"I don't need to change to sit on my sofa and watch movies."

He smiles. "But you're not sitting on your sofa and watching movies. We're going out."

I inhale a deep breath before I shout at Dylan. Shouting at him will not help. "I am not going out."

He scans my living room. "I guess we can invite everyone here, but it's going to be a little crowded."

I throw my arms in the air. "I give up. You're speaking in riddles. Why would I invite anyone into my house?"

"Duh. For your birthday party."

"My birthday isn't for another month."

"Which is how we can make it a surprise." He grins. "Surprise!" He sighs. "Although, you've ruined the surprise now."

I rub my fingers against my temples where I can feel a headache beginning. "Do we have to do this surprise party today?"

"Everything's already set up."

"I'm not really in the mood for a party."

"Don't worry. Cash won't be there."

My heart squeezes and I rub a hand over my chest to alleviate the ache. Cash won't be there? He left Winter Falls already? There go my fantasies of him wallowing in regret for breaking up with me.

Why am I sitting around heartbroken when Cash doesn't even care? I might as well get myself dressed and off to a party.

"Fine," I give in.

"Off you go." Dylan herds me toward the stairs. "Shower, wash your hair, and change your clothes."

"Yes, Mom," I grumble as I follow his orders.

Thirty minutes later, I enter the living room to discover Dylan sitting on the couch next to Katy Purry watching television. I barely recognize the room. The empty containers are missing from the coffee table. The blankets are folded and laid across the back of the couch. It even smells nice in here.

"You cleaned up."

Dylan stands and places the kitty on the floor. He smiles at me. "You look lovely."

Hardly. My cheeks are red and splotchy, my eyes are still puffy from two days of crying, and my curly hair is out of control since I didn't want to spend the time to blow dry it into submission.

"You ready?" He waves toward the door. "Your chariot awaits."

"Where are we going?" I ask once we're in a golf cart.

"To *Electric Vibes*. Where else would we go? It's the only bar in town."

"We could have walked."

"We're running late."

When we enter the bar five minutes later, Clove rushes toward me. "Finally. I thought you'd miss it." She motions to a table in front of the stage where a large television is currently set up.

"Miss what?"

She pushes me forward. What she doesn't do is answer me.

I scowl at Dylan. "This doesn't appear to be a birthday party."

"I might have lied to get you here."

"Dylan." I slap his shoulder. "What's going on?"

He pulls out a chair for me. "Sit down and you'll find out."

"I am never opening my door for you again," I grumble, but I do sit down.

"You'll thank me later."

"I at least deserve a drink."

"Here." Virginia sets a glass of wine on the table.

I sigh. "Thanks."

She smiles as she retreats.

"Where are you going?" I shout after her.

She nods toward Dylan, and I giggle for the first time in days. I may never find love, but I can at least tease my friend about her love/hate relationship with the man sitting next to me.

"Why is she running away?" Dylan asks.

"Hush, everyone! It's starting!" Sage claps her hands to get everyone's attention. Once everyone is focused on her, she switches on the television.

"We're here to watch TV?"

The crowd shushes me. I guess I'm here to watch TV.

The commercial ends and the camera swings to Cash. I stand. I am not watching this. Why would I watch this?

Before I manage one step, Dylan clamps down on my hand to stop me. "Stay." I glare at him. "Please."

"You have five minutes." I collapse back in my chair and cross my arms over my chest. This is ridiculous.

"I'm here today with Cash Evans, the lead singer of *Cash & the Sinners*," the announcer begins.

Cash flashes his trademark smile at him. "Thanks for having me."

"When Cash says he wants to premier his latest song on your show, you make time."

"I appreciate it."

"I understand you want to make an announcement before you begin."

Cash's smile drops and he nods. "I do."

"The world is listening."

"No pressure then." He chuckles. "Every love song I've ever written has been for one girl. My Indy."

I gasp. What is happening?

"I screwed up with her and – before you ask – let me make this clear. Our relationship is private. We won't be sharing any further details with the press. The subject is off limits."

Is Cash announcing our relationship to the world? But he dumped me. I lean forward hoping he'll explain more.

"You're making it difficult for me to ask questions," the host complains.

"I did say this was an announcement."

The host nods as if to concede Cash's point.

"Anyway, I'm here today to sing our upcoming release to my girl and ask her if she'll forgive me."

He picks up his guitar and fiddles with it for a moment before gazing into the camera. I hold my breath as he begins to sing.

I've learned from my mistakes,
I've grown,
And I'll fight for your love,
I've always known,
You're the one I need,

The missing piece of me,
I'm determined to make you see.
I'm gonna win you back,
Prove my love is sincere,
Every moment,
I'll treasure and protect,
With you, I'll resurrect.

It's the song he wrote after the night we kissed on the couch. I fled like a coward from him and he stayed up all night writing a song about getting a second chance. This very song he's singing on national television right now.

Cash steps out from behind the television. He's here? Shouldn't he be in a TV studio somewhere?

Chapter 36

Head up your ass – What happens when you listen to other people instead of your heart

Cash

Indy stares at me with her mouth gaping open. It'd be funny if it weren't for my pulse racing in fear of her rejecting me.

"Indy," I call and she blinks to bring me into focus. "Will you forgive me for being a dumbass?"

"Forgive him! Forgive him!" Dylan begins the chant, but the crowd in the bar is quick to join in.

The five gossip gals climb onto the stage to stand next to me. They insisted on being a part of my apology. It was the only way they'd agree to help set this whole thing up. I'm man enough to admit I'm feeling more than a bit apprehensive over what they have planned.

"One," Sage begins counting off. "Two, three!"

On three, they whip open their sweaters to reveal bright pink t-shirts with the words *Gossip Gals Vote Yes* in gold lettering on them.

"Say yes, Indigo!" Sage shouts.

Feather nods. "He's better than a book boyfriend."

"I'll give you some free massage candles," Petal adds.

Cayenne winks at me. "I'd show him how flexible I can be any day of the week."

Before Clove can speak, I step forward. "I'm sorry, Indy. I let…"

I trail off when the noise in the room cuts off and everyone leans close to listen. Shit. I didn't think this through. I don't want to have this conversation in front of the entire town.

"You can use the storeroom," the bartender hollers.

I don't wait for her to change her mind. I jump off the stage and rush to Indy. She allows me to herd her toward the back hallway and into the storeroom. This is a good sign, right?

Once we're hidden from the crowd behind a closed door, I cradle Indy's face in my hands. "I'm sorry, sweetness. I let your mom's words burrow into my head and I couldn't get them out."

"Head?" She raises her eyebrows. "Don't you mean your ass?"

"Yeah, yeah. My head is up my ass. But it isn't any longer."

"You're not going to run scared every time my mother visits?"

I lock my muscles to stop the shiver at the idea of her mothering visit. Raven may have birthed the woman I love, but she is not a nice person.

"No. But I may hide in the studio whenever she visits."

She studies me and I let her see it all. My love for her, my regret for hurting her, my determination to continue my life with her by my side.

"Good thing dear old mom won't be visiting until she apologizes."

Damn it. I'm still coming between her and her mom. "Indy."

She raises her palm. "Nope. I don't want to hear it."

I blow out a breath and let it go. Discussing Raven will only lead to another fight. And I don't want to fight with Indy.

"Will you give me another chance?"

"How can I compete against a song on the TV?"

"Hey now. It's true I'm a musician, but I'm also just a man. A man who loves you."

She bites her lip. I can see the wheels turning in her head. "How would this even work? You're on the road most of the time. I'll be here in Winter Falls."

"My idiot half-brother pointed out there are these things called phones. We'll speak every day. Maybe we'll even have phone sex." I waggle my eyebrows.

She smacks my shoulder. "I'm serious." She swallows. "There are a lot of temptations on the road."

"No one compares to you, Indy. No one."

She scowls. "You're not taking my concerns seriously."

"I am. Trust me. I am. Besides, we're not touring for at least a year."

"What?"

"We need a break. We're supposed to be on break now, but our producer insisted we get this album done first."

"What about after the year's up?"

I shrug. "We'll figure it out. Do you know if you want to stay in Winter Falls after this year?"

Her nose wrinkles. "No."

I kiss her nose. "Then, we'll figure it out together. And when we go on tour again, you'll visit as often as you can and I'll come home in between shows."

"I don't want you to change your whole life for me."

"You don't get it yet, Indy. I would change everything for you. I'll stop touring altogether if you want."

"The band would resent me."

"No, we won't!" Jett shouts through the door.

She buries her face in my shoulder. "Is everyone listening at the door?"

"Just the band!" Gibson answers.

"And his brothers!" Elder adds.

"Can you forgive him soon?" Brody asks. "I think Soleil's in labor."

"What?" She tears away from me and flings the door open. "Your girlfriend's in labor? What are you doing here?"

Brody grins and points to Soleil at the end of the hallway. "She won't go to the hospital until you forgive Cash."

"I'd forgive a man if he sang a song to me on national television," Soleil says as she waddles closer.

Brody growls at her. "But you won't because you love me and are having my baby."

She shrugs. "It's always good to have a backup plan."

"You should probably forgive him already," Fender says.

Indy plants her hands on her hips and scowls at him. "Why should I listen to you?"

"Cash promised the band would play tonight. And the natives are getting restless." He points toward the crowd at the end of the hallway. Miller is holding them back now but they'll break through soon.

"Fine!" She throws her arms in the air. "I forgive him but if he breaks my heart again, I will come for you. All of you." She points to each of the band members and my brothers in turn.

I shackle her wrist and drag her back into the storeroom. I slam the door closed behind us before pushing her up against a wall. She gasps and I meld my lips to hers. My tongue doesn't wait to invade her mouth. I want to soak up her taste. The taste I've been missing because I'm an idiot.

I'm no longer an idiot. I won't let anything come between us again. Not her mom. Not my fame. She's stuck with me.

Bang! Bang! Bang!

"You promised us a concert, young man."

I slow the kiss until I can pull away. My gaze meets Indy's. "You sure? You're not going to regret this decision?"

"Oh, I'll probably regret this decision a million times when you forget to put the toilet seat down or call my cat a demon or forget to phone one day while you're on the road, but I'm giving you a second chance anyway."

"Thank you, Indy. I love you more than you can ever know."

"I love you, too, Cash."

"I'm going to prove to you that you made the right decision."

"I hope the proof begins with this." She rubs her hand over my hard cock and I moan.

"Concert now! Sexy times later!"

Indy giggles at Dylan's shout. "Why did you promise them a concert tonight?"

I shrug. "I want the people of Winter Falls to like me. This is our home after all."

"We'll like you better if you start singing!" Sage hollers.

I chuckle as I take Indy's hand and lead her toward the door. She drags her feet.

"Don't you want to wait?" She nods toward my crotch.

"I'm not staying in here all night." Which is how long it will take for this erection to go down. When Indy's around, my cock is ready to go.

She giggles again, and I kiss her hair.

"For you Indy, I'll do anything."

I'll repeat those words until she realizes how true they are.

Chapter 37

Virginia – A woman whose patience is up

VIRGINIA

I frown at the entrance to *Electric Vibes.* A bar is not where I want to spend my time. I had a lovely evening planned. A new book from Lucy Score and a glass of wine. I don't need more.

Instead, I'm being dragged to a bar of all places. I don't do bars. They're too loud with blaring music. And they're full of people.

Maybe I'm being a bit melodramatic. I haven't been literally dragged here. I'm here to support my friend. I'd do anything for the woman who shielded me from bullies in high school. Even come to a noisy bar.

I can do this. I straighten my back and walk inside. When the noise hits me, I nearly turn around.

But I catch sight of Indigo sitting in front of the stage. She appears the definition of unhappy. I can't blame her. I'm not happy to be at the bar today and I didn't get my heart broken by the love of my life.

I snatch a glass of wine from a tray – the least I can do for her is make sure she has a drink – as I make my way across the bar to her. I nearly stumble when I notice who she's sitting with.

Dylan. The jerk who won't stop asking me out.

If he had asked me out in high school, I would have screamed yes. But he never noticed me back then. In fact, he doesn't remember me from high school at all. Ouch.

I'll give Indigo her drink and then get far, far away from Mr. Forgetful.

"Here you go," I say as I hand the wine to Indigo.

Dylan smiles at me and my knees wobble. Dang him! And my stupid body!

Retreat! Retreat! Retreat!

I manage to smile at Indigo before fleeing. I won't leave. Considering what's about to happen, Indigo may very well need me. But I refuse to be in Dylan's presence.

I hide in the corner of the bar with a glass of wine while Cash does the biggest grand gesture known to man. It's beyond romantic. If I were Indigo, I would have forgiven him right away. But that's not my friend. She made Cash work for his second chance.

Once the drama's over, *Cash & the Sinners* take the stage. Apparently, Cash agreed to put on a concert in return for the town's help with his grand gesture.

"Good evening, Winter Falls," Cash begins.

The gossip gals rush to the front of the stage and scream in response to his intro. Those women scare the snot out of me.

They're old enough to be my grandmother but they certainly don't act like my grandma.

Time for me to go home. Indigo and Cash are back together. Their happily ever after is secured. My book is calling my name.

I'm nearly at the door when Indigo clamps a hand down on my shoulder. "And where do you think you're going?"

Instead of answering her question, I draw her into a hug. "I'm happy for you, Indigo."

She giggles and sways me from side to side. "I can't believe what just happened."

"You deserve it." She was broken when Cash dumped her at our high school graduation. I'm glad they've found their way back to each other.

"You could have this, too, you know." She tries to guide me toward the stage but I plant my feet and refuse to budge.

"He doesn't remember who I am," I hiss.

"So, tell him."

I scowl at her. Tell Dylan we went to high school together? Great idea. Then, he'll know what a complete loser I am. A mouse he didn't bother to notice for four years of high school.

"Whatever you're thinking is wrong."

The band starts playing making it impossible to continue this conversation. Time to escape.

But there is no escape for me. Indigo must have super strength because she drags me toward the stage. I wish I was the person who would kick and scream until she let me go. But I'm not. I'm the girl who doesn't raise her voice.

"Suck it up, buttercup!" Indigo shouts when we reach the front of the crowd.

I try to inch backwards but there's nowhere to go. The crowd surges toward the stage. If I want to escape, I'll have to go against them. Which is not happening. Being shy and introverted sucks sometimes.

"This song is for Indy, the love of my life," Cash announces.

I try to keep my eyes pinned to Cash. I really do. But before I know what's happening, my gaze drifts to Dylan.

He was cute in high school, but now? Now, he's as sexy as any book boyfriend I could ever imagine.

His gaze meets mine and he winks. I bet he's winked at a thousand women in the crowd before. I roll my eyes and he grins.

As the band plays, I'm ashamed to admit, I can't keep my eyes off Dylan. Is there anything sexier than a man playing the guitar? The muscles in his biceps and forearms contract as he plays and my fingers itch to touch them. To feel how hard those muscles are. Is his skin soft to the touch?

His right arm sports a full sleeve of tattoos. I never thought I'd find tattoos sexy, but I'm intrigued by his ink. What does it mean? How would he react if I traced every inch with my tongue?

"We're going to take a small break," Cash announces after the fifth song.

The crowd begins to disperse and Indigo makes her way toward Cash. This is my chance to escape.

The front door is too far away and there are too many people blocking me. I march toward the back entrance instead.

"Virginia, hold up!"

I pretend I don't hear Dylan shout and keep moving. Unfortunately, I must be too slow since his big hand comes down on my shoulder and whirls me around.

"Hey, Virginia." He smiles.

"I'm leaving." I hate how rude I sound but I'm weak for this man. And I refuse to be weak for a man who ignored my existence in high school.

His hand travels from my shoulder to my neck where his thumb rubs circles into my skin. Sparks go off in my body and I gasp.

"You feel it, too."

I wrench away from him and his magic hands. "I don't know what you're referring to."

He smirks. "A challenge? I do love a challenge."

He thinks I'm a challenge? He doesn't view me as a woman he wants to spend time with, to get to know. Nope. All I am is a game to him. Too bad for him I refuse to be another notch in his bedpost.

"I am not a challenge. I am a woman."

He holds up his hands. "I didn't—"

I poke him in the chest. "You treat women like they're a competition you're determined to win. Women aren't games."

"You have the wrong opinion of me. I'm not Jett who treats sex like a drug or Gibson who gets a kick out of charming a woman into bed."

Thanks for the reminder. He's a rockstar who could never be truly interested in a quiet librarian in a small town.

"I'm leaving." I whirl around but before I can get away, he shackles my wrist to stop me.

Oh no, he didn't! I may be a quiet woman but I will not put up with a man ordering me where I can go or not go.

I wrench my hand free. "Do not touch me without my permission."

Never mind he touched my neck and I enjoyed it. This is different. He's trying to stop me from leaving. No one can stop me from going where I want to go. Never again.

He retreats a step. "Sorry. It was a mistake."

It was a mistake! Those four words are my least favorite in the English vocabulary. I've heard enough of 'it was a mistake' and 'I didn't mean to' for the rest of my life.

"I just wanted to get a chance to ask you out before you go home."

"Buy a clue, Dylan! I will never go out with you!"

I spin around and stomp toward the exit. I can feel my face flaming with shame. I know better than to raise my voice. I know what the consequences can be.

No. Not anymore. There will be no consequences. That part of my life is over and done.

The door opens behind me and I glance back over my shoulder. It's Dylan.

"Leave me alone!"

"I'm not letting you walk home alone and angry."

"You're not walking me home."

"I'll walk behind you. You don't need to speak to me, but I need to make sure you get home safe."

Damn him. He had to say the magic words? There's nothing I want more than a man who can make me feel safe.

But Dylan is not that man.

Chapter 38

Biology – Doesn't always mean anything when it comes to a parent

INDIGO

I pace in front of the living room window. I hear a door shut and rush to look outside. Nope. No visitor has arrived.

Cash wraps his arms around my waist. "What's going on Indy?"

"Nothing."

He chuckles. "Liar."

I whirl around to face him. "Why do you think I'm a liar?"

He nods toward my hands where I'm cracking my knuckles. Shoot. I hide my hands behind my back. "I'm not lying."

"Why are you nervous?"

Because I did something very scary and I'm worried he's going to be mad at me. I hate when Cash is mad at me. Although make-up sex is pretty spectacular. Something to look forward to.

"What makes you think I'm nervous?"

"You've spent the last thirty minutes pacing the living room."

I check the clock. He should have been here by now. The doorbell rings and I jump.

Cash starts for the door, but I stop him. "Let me. And please don't be mad at me."

"If it's your mom, I need to book some studio time," he mutters.

It's not my mom. The opposite in fact.

I open the door. "Hi, Dad."

He hugs me tight and I inhale his scent. I missed him. "Hi, baby girl."

He releases me and I smile up at him. "I'm glad you're here."

"Sorry it took me so long."

I nod in understanding and motion toward Cash who's hovering at the entrance to the living room. "You remember Cash?"

Dad extends his hand. "I expect you to ask me for her hand in marriage before you propose."

"Dad!" I slap his stomach. "Cash isn't proposing."

"I'm not?" Cash asks.

My cheeks warm and I sputter. "N-n-not right this second."

He winks. "Okay. I'll wait."

"You're impossible."

He chuckles. "And you love me."

My cheeks are now at nuclear level. I can't believe he said the L-word in front of my dad.

"I'm going to bring in Dad's suitcases."

"Suitcases?" Cash asks as he follows me.

Uh oh. This is the part he's going to be mad about.

I avoid his gaze as I answer. "Um…Dad's moving in with us."

"Thank fuck." He grabs a suitcase from me. "When you insisted on building a mother-in-law suite for 'guests', I thought you meant your mom."

"My mother is not welcome in this house until she apologizes to you."

"Hell will freeze over first," Dad says.

"True story," I mutter.

Dad reaches for a suitcase, but Cash dances out of his way. "I've got these. Go relax. There's coffee in the kitchen."

I follow Cash to the mother-in-law suite. I close the door behind us so Dad can't hear.

"Are you okay with Dad moving in here?"

"He's still divorcing your mom?"

I nod. Once the real reason Mom hates Cash came out – namely, she slept with his biological father when I was in elementary school and was devastated when he didn't want more than one night – Dad couldn't divorce Mom quick enough.

"Good."

I don't know about good. "How sad is it that I'm glad my parents are divorcing?"

Cash cradles my face. "Sweetness, do not beat yourself up. You want your dad to be happy. This is the way it has to happen."

The doorbell rings.

"Let's go see who decided to invade first." Cash kisses my nose before leading me to the entrance.

Dad already has the door open. I peek past him to see who it is. Uh oh. The gossip gals are here.

"What do you want?" I ask.

The gossip gals answer by shoving their way into our home.

"Is this your dad?" Sage asks.

I guess I'm doing introductions. "Dad, this is the gossip gals. Feather, Petal, Sage, Cayenne, and Clove. This is my father, Ethan."

"Ladies." Dad smiles at them. "To what do I owe this pleasure?"

Sage crosses her arms over her chest. "We haven't decided if this is a pleasure yet."

"We need to make sure you're not here to run our boy Cash out of Winter Falls," Feather adds.

"I would never," Dad claims.

Petal purses her lips. "Your wife did."

He sighs. "She did, but she's not my wife anymore."

Clove pokes him. "Being divorced doesn't mean you don't agree with her."

"No, but moving in with Cash and my daughter does."

Feather gasps. "You're moving to Winter Falls?"

"He already has. His stuff is in his room." I motion down the hallway to where his bedroom is.

"Gossip gals, we need to confer." Sage herds the women across the room where they huddle together.

"I'm sorry, Dad," I whisper my apology since those women have excellent hearing.

He grins. "After what your mother did, I'm glad someone's sticking up for Cash."

"But they're being rude."

"I don't think they're rude. I think they're lovely." He glances across the room to where the gossip gals are standing. He catches Feather's eye and winks at her. "Excuse me. I should offer our guests a drink."

I groan as I watch him saunter over to the women.

"What's wrong?" Cash asks.

"I think my dad has the hots for one of the gossip gals."

His response? He barks out a laugh.

I elbow him. "It's not funny. The gossip gals are a menace."

He wraps an arm around me and hauls me close. "Maybe if they're busy matchmaking one of their own, they'll leave the rest of us alone."

"I don't know. They have a lot of energy. And time on their hands."

"I like them."

"Because they hurried over here to protect you. They didn't need to invade the house. I would have protected you."

He kisses my hair. "I know. But it's nice to be welcomed into the community."

"Has anyone made you feel unwelcome? Who? I'll handle it."

He bursts into laughter. And since he's holding me, I get the chance to feel his humor. I enjoy it for a moment before I shove him away.

"Are you saying I can't handle it?" I motion toward my dad. "Why do you think I asked him to come live here?"

He sobers. "You asked your dad to move to Winter Falls? Why?"

"Duh." I roll my eyes. "Dad needed somewhere to go after the divorce and you've always wanted a dad." I shrug. "I figured we could share mine."

"Sweetness," he murmurs before his lips slam down on mine. I gasp in surprise and he uses the opportunity to push his tongue into my mouth. His taste hits me and I moan. I also forget all about our visitors until they start hooting and hollering.

"Find a room!"

"Go, Cash!"

"I'd let him stick his tongue down my throat!"

I bury my red face into Cash's neck. He wraps his arms tight around me.

"Thank you, Indy," Cash whispers into my hair. "Thank you for giving me a second chance and for loving me the way you do."

"You're welcome," I mutter into his shirt.

I hear feet shuffling behind me before Dad announces, "The ladies are taking me on a tour of the town. We'll be gone for at least an hour."

I wait until the door shuts behind them before I lift my head. "Did that just happen?"

"Did what just happen?"

"Did my dad leave so we can have sex?"

Cash picks me up and cradles me in his arms. "We shouldn't waste a moment of time."

"You're lucky I love you, Cash Evans."

He stops and glances down at me. "I am lucky you love me. I'm the luckiest man in the world. And now I'm going to make you the luckiest woman in the world."

"You already did. You already did."

D.E. Haggerty

Love and Laughter In Every Chapter

About the Author

D.E. Haggerty is an American who has spent the majority of her adult life abroad. She has lived in Istanbul, various places throughout Germany, and currently finds herself in The Hague. She has been a military policewoman, a lawyer, a B&B owner/operator and now a writer.

Printed in Dunstable, United Kingdom

80665512R00167